Riana

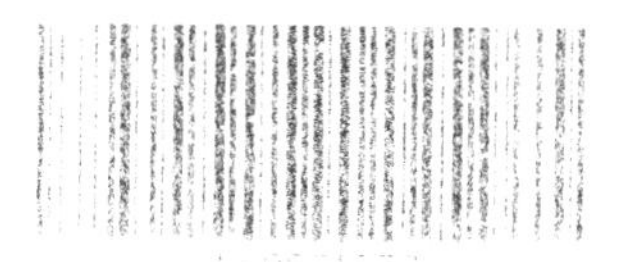

Cassie and the Devil's Charm

Terrance Dicks lives in North London. He has written many books for Piccadilly Press including the Changing Universe series, the Unexplained series, the Chronicles of a Computer Addict series, the Harvey series and The Good, The Bad and the Ghastly series.

Second Sight

Cassie and the Devil's Charm

Terrance Dicks

First published in Great Britain in 2000
by Piccadilly Press Ltd.,
5 Castle Road, London NW1 8PR

Phototypeset from author's disc
in 12.25/17.5 pt Bembo

A catalogue record for this book is available
from the British Library

ISBN: 1 85340 632 5 (paperback)
1 85340 637 6 (hardback)

1 3 5 7 9 10 8 6 4 2

Printed and bound by
Creative Print and Design (Wales),
Ebbw Vale

Design & cover design by Judith Robertson

CHAPTER ONE

CRASH

The first time I saw Cassie Sinclair was on the Thursday afternoon of the week before half-term.

She was standing in the entrance of the school bus, clinging firmly to the sides of the door.

I heard a clear, determined voice floating across the square that divided the two school buildings.

'I won't go. I won't get on. You can't make me!'

The bus was parked outside the main door of the girls' school building. From just inside the open coach door an agitated teacher was trying to calm things down. Behind Cassie a straggling line of girls was muttering impatient protests.

'What's going on?'

'We're going to be late!'

'Somebody shift her!'

It was none of my business of course. But then there was the girl. She was about a year younger than me, fifteen or so, quite tall and thin, all arms and legs. She had a high forehead, big green eyes and long fair hair. She was the most beautiful thing I'd ever seen. She looked . . . vulnerable.

I went over to her. 'Something wrong? Can I help?'

Although the boys' and girls' sections of the school were in different buildings, I knew the teacher. Her name was Miss Prendergast. Tall and thin and beaky-nosed, she was the old-fashioned type, which probably wasn't helping.

'It's this silly girl here, Cassandra Sinclair,' she butted in. 'She's new this term. She's got some ridiculous idea about not going on the museum trip.'

I gave the girl a friendly grin. She scowled back at me.

'She'd better not go, then,' I suggested.

'But she has to go,' snapped Miss Prendergast. 'We're late already! Besides, it's down on the timetable!'

She made the timetable sound as sacred as the ten commandments. I suppose it was to her.

I kept my voice calm and reasonable. 'There's no point in trying to make her go if she doesn't want to.'

'But she's in my class, I'm responsible for her!' Her voice rose angrily. 'We have to leave *right now* or we'll be late, and she's clearly in no state to be left alone.'

'I'll look after her if you like,' I offered. 'Take her back to school, hand her over to another teacher.'

Miss Prendergast looked hard at me. 'I know you, don't I, young man?'

'Ben Harker, Miss Prendergast. I'm in your drama group.'

As I said, the male and female sections of the school are strictly segregated. But there are one or two joint activities – like the choir and the drama groups. It is rumoured, perish the thought, that some people actually joined these groups just to meet members of the opposite sex.

Miss Prendergast gave me a considering look. 'You seem to be a reasonably responsible boy. Take her back into school and hand her over to her form teacher, Mrs Bell. Perhaps Cassandra can explain her behaviour to her.'

I took the girl's arm and gently detached her from the door frame.

'It's all right, you don't have to go,' I said soothingly. 'Come and sit down and we'll sort things out.'

I led her away from the bus towards one of the stone benches that line the quad.

Behind us I could hear Miss Prendergast rallying the troops. 'Now come along, girls, take your places on the bus in an orderly fashion. This delay has cost us far too much time as it is!'

When we reached the bench the girl sat down, hugging herself. She was quivering like a guitar string.

'What's it all about, then?' I asked. 'I mean, I know a visit to the British Museum isn't a bundle of laughs, but aren't you carrying the protest a bit far?'

Her reply amazed me.

'I saw the crash,' she whispered. 'Saw the bus turn over. I could hear them screaming.'

I couldn't make any sense of what she was saying.

'Saw what crash? Where?' An idea struck me. 'You mean you had a dream?'

She shook her head. 'You don't understand. Nobody understands. I saw it when I touched the bus doorway.' She looked up at me, her eyes full of a kind of angry appeal. 'That bus is going to crash, I know it is!'

I looked down at her in puzzlement, wondering what on earth I'd taken on.

'Ah, right . . .' I thought for a moment. 'Why not warn them, then? If you're so sure . . .'

Her head drooped and her shoulders slumped. 'They wouldn't believe me,' she muttered. 'Nobody ever believes me.'

I just stood there for a moment, staring down at the top of her head. She was weird – but she was still beautiful. It struck me that if I could reassure her somehow, she might feel better.

'I've got an idea,' I said. 'You stay here. Promise?'

She nodded and I turned and ran back to the bus.

I was just in time to catch them before the bus set off. Everyone was seated by now, and the coach driver was just about to slam the door. He stopped when I came running up.

'You coming too? Jump in with the other girls!'

He was a flash-looking type with a shaved head and a stubbly chin. A real comedian. Ignoring him, I turned to Miss Prendergast. She'd bagged the front passenger seat, the way teachers always do.

She gave me a severe look. 'What is it, Ben? We're just about to set off.'

'I thought you might like to know what was bothering the girl.'

'Well?'

'Apparently she saw this telly documentary not long ago. Something about a series of coach crashes. A lot of kids got badly hurt because they weren't wearing seat belts.'

'I can assure you that this coach is fitted with passenger seat belts,' said Miss Prendergast frostily.

'So were some of the coaches that crashed. People don't always bother to put them on.'

'They will on this one!' said Miss Prendergast grimly. 'Now, if that's all – we're very late.'

'That's partly why I mentioned it,' I said. 'I wouldn't trust this character to drive a hearse, and if he tries to cut corners . . .'

'You what?' said the driver.

He raised a hand as if to clip my ear and made a grab at me but Miss Prendergast soon sorted him out.

'That's quite enough of that,' she said sharply. 'You'd better be going, Ben.'

As I turned away from the coach, I heard the teacher's raised voice. 'Now then, girls, seat belts will be worn. Fasten them now. I shall be coming round to check in a moment. And, driver, please drive carefully.'

The door slammed and the coach roared away.

I went back to the bench and sat down next to the girl. She seemed a bit more cheerful now.

She looked up and said simply, 'Thanks.'

I held out my hand. 'Ben Harker. And you're – Cassandra?'

'Cassie,' she said quickly. 'I hate that name. Call me Cassie.'

'I know how you feel,' I said. 'I'm not mad about Benjamin!'

Cassie had other reasons for disliking her full name, but I didn't find that out until later. Solemnly we shook hands. Her hand felt thin and delicate inside mine. I held it briefly and then let go.

In a way, Cassie's appearance was deceptive. In spite of her leggy, Bambi-like air, she was a lot tougher than she looked, as I soon learned.

Suddenly she frowned.

'What's up?' I asked.

'The coach. I can't help worrying.'

'Maybe it'll be all right,' I said. I told her the tale I'd spun Miss Prendergast.

She looked thoughtfully at me. 'That was very – inventive of you.'

'A polite way to put it,' I said. 'You might say I'm a naturally good liar.'

She laughed. 'Do you often make up stories like that?'

'Sometimes. When the truth gets a bit too boring – or too inconvenient.'

It was true enough. I had a bad habit of spinning tall tales just for the fun of it. Sometimes it got me into trouble. Sometimes, like now, it came in very handy.

Cassie went on looking happy for a moment, then that frown came back. She glanced at the school building. 'I guess we'd better go in and report to Mrs Bell.'

I grinned at her. 'Whatever for? As far as anyone knows you're on the museum trip, right? And that takes up the last two periods of the day. Let's go for a walk.'

'What about you? Shouldn't you be in school?'

'I'm on a free period right now. Next period's Maths, and I'm rubbish at Maths.'

'But we'll get into trouble.'

'What's wrong with a bit of trouble in a good cause?'

'But Miss Prendergast said –'

'You don't always have to do what other people tell you,' I said gently.

She thought about this revolutionary idea for a moment, then jumped to her feet. 'All right, let's go!'

We set off across the campus.

We'd just passed the boys' building when we heard a voice behind us.

'And where are you two off to, may I ask?'

I turned and saw Mr Paine, the deputy head coming down the steps. Like Miss Prendergast he was one of the old school: tall, thin, bespectacled and suspicious.

'This is Cassandra Sinclair, sir, she's a new girl. She got sick before the museum trip, and Miss Prendergast asked me to look after her, so I'm seeing her home. I'm on a free period at the moment.'

Old Paine considered this suspiciously.

'She really isn't very well, sir,' I added helpfully. 'She was afraid she was going to be sick. She still feels pretty queasy, sir.'

Mr Paine shuddered in horror at the thought of anyone throwing up on his sacred school square. He looked uneasily at Cassie, who really was looking pretty sick by now.

'Very well, be off with you. I hope you soon feel better, young lady.'

'Thank you,' whispered Cassie.

As we walked through the main gate she said, 'I can see why you're rubbish at Maths.'

'Really? Why?'

'My father says mathematics is the home of absolute truth. That wouldn't suit you at all!'

As we went on our way, Cassie looked up at the old grey stone buildings surrounding the central campus.

'It's quite a place, this. Intimidating.'

'It's not too bad when you get used to it.' Actually, I was quite fond of the old place.

The distinguished educational establishment from which we were about to bunk off was St John's Academy for the Sons and Daughters of Gentlefolk.

It's in the heart of the City of London, and it was founded back when Dick Whittington was Lord Mayor of London. There's even a legend that it was actually founded *by* Dick Whittington, although the evidence for that is a bit shaky. Still it makes a nice story for the parents who fork out for the school's high fees.

The academy still keeps up its connections with the City, but these days it's basically a posh public school for the sons and daughters of the well-heeled.

Like my father.

I was thinking about him as we walked through the main arch and out into the City streets.

Suddenly Cassie said, 'What does your father do?'

It was as though she was reading my mind. At the time I thought it was just a coincidence. But, as I discovered later, she had a weird habit of somehow tuning in to your thoughts.

I shrugged. 'Oh, you know. Something in the City. Merchant banker, financial tycoon. In the office by eight o'clock, home on the stroke of ten. Unless he's working late, of course.'

I was exaggerating, but not much.

'He's abroad at the moment,' I added.

'And your mother?'

'I never really had one.'

'Dead?' asked Cassie sympathetically.

I shook my head. 'No, she's still going strong. She was some kind of society beauty. She married Dad when he made his first million.'

'What happened?'

'I told you the way Dad works. He was busy making his next few millions and I suppose she got tired of a life of lonely luxury. Not long after I was born, she went off to find herself. As far as I know she's still looking.'

'Do you ever see her?'

'Occasionally. We get on quite well.'

Cassie looked shocked and sympathetic at the same time.

'How did you end up here, at St John's?'

'Last resort, really. I passed through several schools fairly rapidly. The last one was one of those free school places: no rules, everyone equal, work if you felt like it.'

Cassie smiled. 'Sounds just right for you.'

I shook my head. 'I hated it.'

'Why?'

I grinned. 'You can't be a rebel and a rule-breaker when there are no rules to break. Takes all the fun out of things. How can you beat the system when there's no system to beat?'

Strangely enough, dear old St John's suited me fine. Old-fashioned values. Hard work and discipline. A real challenge. Anything you got away with there you were *really* getting away with!

'What about your lot?' I asked. 'Family, I mean.'

'Dad's a professor of law at Cambridge. He married Mum when she was his brightest and best student. Then she graduated, went out into the world and became a high-flying barrister.'

'"I object, me lud. My client is clearly innocent!" That sort of thing?'

Cassie smiled. 'Occasionally. Mostly she's involved in high finance. Contract and corporation law. She hardly ever appears in Court.'

'And your father?'

'Still in Cambridge. He specialises in History of Law. He's not really interested in anything much later than the *Magna Carta*.'

'Are they separated?'

Cassie shook her head. 'No, they're just separate. They're quite fond of each other, actually, they just don't meet very often.'

We'd been walking along together without taking much notice of where we were heading. Suddenly I realised we were at my building – an enormous, old-fashioned block of luxury flats. Three blocks, actually, in a sort of square U-shape, with raised walkways linking the separate towers.

'We're at Pennington Towers!'

Cassie nodded. 'That's where I live.'

'There's a coincidence.'

'You too?'

'Me too.'

'How come I've never seen you?' asked Cassie.

'We only moved in a few weeks ago. We used to live in the Barbican, but this is handy for the school and Dad's office.'

Cassie nodded. 'Same for me and Mum.'

Pennington Towers was built sometime in the Thirties as the latest thing in luxury flats. It was a huge, rambling place with miles of corridors and innumerable courtyards and gardens. Restaurants, cafés, shops, a swimming-pool and a gym were all built-in. There were resident cleaners and caretakers. You could live in there and never need to go out. Recently restored and refurbished, it was as trendy as ever.

I looked at Cassie and realised I didn't want her to get away.

'Well, here we are,' I said. 'Fancy a coffee or a Coke?'

'All right.'

There was a nice little Italian café in the garden round the back. We sat outside under a striped umbrella drinking *café latte* and chatting for about an hour. We got on really well. Neither of us mentioned her worries about the coach trip or her crazy idea about getting flashes of the future. Finally Cassie said she ought to be getting back. We arranged to meet next morning at the main entrance and walk to school together – it turned out we lived in different blocks.

I was still thinking about her as I made my way back to our penthouse flat.

A real beauty, I thought. That hair and those big green eyes. Even though she seemed a bit shy and vulnerable, I could already sense a really strong character underneath. Once she relaxed, she was funny and smart as well. She was going to be very popular when word got round.

I decided I'd been lucky to meet her early on, while she was still fairly new to the school. I made a rapid review of my friends and decided she was too good for any of them.

It was a shame she was a bit crazy, of course, but then you can't have everything. Maybe her mother told her too many ghost stories when she was little.

At least, that's what I thought – until I watched the local news on telly later that night. There was a story about a school bus crash, near the British Museum, with a picture of the overturned bus. That comedian of a driver must have tried to cut corners after all. The driver had been hurt, but the teacher and pupils had all escaped with minor cuts and bruises.

Unlike the unfortunate driver, they'd all been wearing their seat belts.

CHAPTER TWO

Unwanted Gift

When I met Cassie next morning outside Pennington Towers the worried look was back in full force.

'See the news?' I asked.

She nodded without speaking, looking anxiously at me.

'All right,' I said. 'I take it all back!'

'Take what back? You didn't say anything.'

'Not what I was saying – what I was thinking.'

'You thought I was crazy,' she accused. Somehow it was as if she'd picked the word out of my mind.

'Well, over-imaginative, anyway. Does this sort of thing happen to you often?'

'Sometimes,' she said solemnly. 'Too often for comfort.'

'It's not too long till the Grand National,' I said hopefully.

She shook her head. 'It's never anything nice – or useful. I might be able to tell you which horse was going to fall, or which jockey was going to break his neck.'

'Always bad news?'

'Nearly always. Look, you won't tell anyone, will you?'

I shook my head. 'Not a word.'

'Only, I had a bad time at my last school,' she went on. 'People thought I was weird. I wanted it to be different here.' She sighed. 'Fat chance of that now.'

'Why?'

'After all the fuss I made yesterday?'

'Stick with that story I told Miss Prendergast,' I suggested. 'Or just say you hate coach rides because you get travel-sick. Say you threw up over a teacher at your last school and you were terrified it would happen again.'

She laughed. It was nice to see her laugh.

'I haven't got your rich imagination!'

'Don't worry about it,' I said. 'I'll make up the tales and you can tell them. We'll make a good team.'

'Yes,' she said seriously. 'I think we will.'

We set off for school.

'That's some gift you've got there,' I said as we walked along.

Cassie shook her head. 'It's not a gift, it's a curse. Imagine what it's like, knowing that bad things are going to happen and not being able to do anything about it.'

'You could warn people.'

'I've tried but nobody listens. Either that or they just don't believe me. Until you. I feel so helpless – and guilty.'

'Why guilty?'

'For not helping.'

'You helped yesterday,' I pointed out. 'I'm pretty certain that warning I passed on made Miss Prendergast more careful. That's why everyone was wearing their seat belts. Otherwise the accident could have been a whole lot worse.'

'*You* helped,' she said. 'I was useless, as usual.'

'*We* helped,' I said firmly. 'You provided the information, I passed it on – slightly altered.'

She didn't look convinced.

'Is it always like yesterday?' I asked. 'Sudden flashes near the time?'

She shook her head. 'Sometimes there are dreams.

Sometimes I just get feelings about things, or places. About people sometimes, what they're really like.'

She looked hard at me, and I started feeling uneasy.

I tried to make a joke of it. 'How am I doing?'

'Very well,' she said. 'You're the only honest liar I've ever met!'

For some reason I felt absurdly pleased.

We walked on for a bit in silence.

Suddenly Cassie said, 'Mum's having a sort of cocktail party thing tonight, she often does on Fridays. Do you think you could come?'

'I suppose so,' I said doubtfully. 'I'm not really the cocktail party type.'

'Please,' she said. 'There's someone I want you to meet.' She looked at me appealingly with those big green eyes and my heart turned over.

'Yes, of course I'll come,' I said. 'It'll be a pleasure.'

She wouldn't tell me any more, though. She wouldn't even tell me who she wanted me to meet.

Six o'clock that evening found me on my way over to Cassie's flat. Like ours, it was one of the top-floor penthouses, which meant that her family, like mine, wasn't short of a few quid.

I was all dressed up, in honour of the occasion, in a black shirt and black Paul Smith trousers. That's as dressed up as I get. Not even Cassie was going to get me into a suit.

I came out of the lift, walked along the lavishly carpeted corridor and rang the bell. Believe it or not, a maid, an actual maid in black dress and white apron opened the door. I didn't think they still existed, outside old movies on telly. She gave me a suspicious look.

'Yes?'

'I'm here for the party.'

'Do you have an invitation?'

'Yes, I do,' I said, stepping past her into the hallway. 'I'm a guest of Miss Sinclair. Tell her I'm here. Please.'

She looked more inclined to tell the police, but luckily Cassie appeared from a doorway at the end of the hall.

'It's all right,' she called. 'This is a friend of mine.'

The maid wasn't convinced. 'I'm not sure if –'

'I said it's all right!' There was an authority in Cassie's voice that sent the maid scurrying away down the hall. 'Sorry about that,' she said. 'I should have warned her you were coming. We've got a few minor celebs here and everyone's a bit security conscious.'

'My own fault for looking like a stalker!'

'You look very handsome,' she said, and my heart did another of those somersaults.

It suddenly struck me that I was getting it bad. I like

to think I'm not the susceptible type – but she really was *very* pretty.

Cassie herself was wearing a simple blue dress. She looked neat, elegant, formal, and thoroughly uncomfortable.

Once again she read my mind. 'Not me, is it? I hate it. But it keeps Mum quiet.'

'You look terrific,' I said. I meant it too. With her thin elegant shape she was a natural model. She'd have looked terrific in an old sack.

Cassie blushed; she looked as if she didn't get too many compliments.

'Nice of you to say so. Come and meet Mother and the guests.'

'Must we? How about sneaking out for a pizza?'

'Certainly not,' said Cassie firmly. 'Come along.'

I looked into those big green eyes.

I came along.

I could hear a buzz of voices, growing louder as we went along the hall. She led me into a large, luxuriously furnished, split-level room. On the far side was a huge window with a stunning view over the City.

The room was full of well-dressed, trendy-looking people all clutching glasses and talking nineteen to the dozen. Some of them may even have been listening, but I doubt it.

I recognised a few politicians, an actor or two and a scattering of the sort of people you know you've seen on telly sometime, though you're not quite sure when.

The rest were serious-looking men and women in serious suits, presumably the high-powered lawyers, financiers and businessmen who made up Cassie's mother's world.

White-coated waiters carried trays of drinks round, and dark-uniformed girls circulated with more trays of incredibly complicated titbits made from smoked salmon, caviar and similarly expensive food.

I saw at once that staff, food and drink all came from one of the many high-priced catering agencies that dealt with this sort of affair. You laid out the cash and they laid it all on. Dad had used this particular outfit himself – I even recognised some of the waitresses.

I'd been to one or two similar events with Dad before I dug my heels in and started refusing to go. It was exactly the sort of occasion I hate. I nearly bolted for freedom, but Cassie did it again. She read my mind.

'I know,' she said quietly. 'I feel exactly the same. Please stay. It's really important.'

So I stayed.

She led me across the room to where a neat, dark-haired woman was talking to a circle of serious suits. They were hanging like limpets to her every word.

She looked up as we approached, excused herself, and came towards us.

'This is Ben Harker, Mum,' said Cassie. 'We met at school yesterday.'

'How do you do, Mrs Sinclair?' I said in my best party voice.

Mrs Sinclair – somehow I felt it really ought to be Ms – gave me a firm handshake and a meaningless social smile.

'You're the young man who was so kind to Cassie when she had her little upset yesterday.'

As she spoke she was sizing me up, checking out the manner, the accent and the clothes of her daughter's new friend. I didn't like it much. I didn't like the belittling way she talked about Cassie either.

'It was a pretty fortunate upset, considering what happened to that coach,' I said. 'Cassie's got a good instinct. She'd make a good business consultant.'

Mrs Sinclair gave me a tolerant smile. 'Following instinct is hardly the way we make decisions in business.'

'Maybe you should start,' I said. 'The way most business managers perform, they'd do better using tea leaves.'

Her eyes widened a little. Clearly she wasn't used to

her daughter's friends talking back, and didn't much care for it.

'That's your opinion, is it?'

I smiled sweetly at her. 'My father's actually.'

Mrs Sinclair dismissed the subject. She'd got no idea who my father was, and she obviously didn't care.

'And do you live near here, Ben?'

'Couldn't be nearer,' said Cassie. 'Ben lives here in Pennington Towers, too.'

Mrs Sinclair's social instincts became alert again.

'You're here as well, are you?' she asked casually. 'Whereabouts?'

'North Tower,' I said equally casually. 'Penthouse. Cassie and I can wave to each other from our windows.'

Her eyes widened again. North Tower was the poshest part of this very posh complex.

She frowned. 'You did say Harker? You must be Simon Harker's boy. I worked on some contracts once, for one of your father's companies. I don't suppose he'd remember. We never actually met.'

My position on the social stock market had clearly shot right up. I liked it about as much as I'd liked the maid taking me for a celebrity-stalker.

Mrs Sinclair saw my reaction and suddenly came over all human. 'Sorry, Ben, it's a kind of professional reflex, networking, checking people out. Sad, isn't it?

I'm impressed about your father, but it really doesn't matter. Any friend of Cassie's is welcome here. Now, if you'll forgive me . . .' She gave me another smile, a real one this time, and I found myself liking her a little. She wasn't too big on warmth and charm, but at least she was honest in her way. She nodded to us both and went back to mingling with her VIP guests.

Cassie led me over to the corner bar and we got a couple of mineral waters.

I'd intended to try to make a good impression, though I'd probably blown it already.

'What did you make of her?' asked Cassie.

'Very – impressive.'

'She didn't seem to impress you all that much!'

I groaned. 'Big-mouth strikes again! I wasn't rude, was I?'

'No, I think she liked you,' said Cassie seriously. 'Mum's so competitive she tries to dominate everyone she meets. Anyone she can do it to she despises immediately!'

Suddenly, looking over my shoulder, she stiffened. I turned in the direction of her gaze and saw a tall, broad-shouldered man with a heavy moustache coming into the room. He wore an expensive suit that made the others in the room look tatty and had a classically handsome, deeply tanned face that made me ready to hate him before meeting him.

Behind him in a little group came three dark-suited men. One was small and scrawny, one tall and thin, one burly and thuggish. All three had moustaches, presumably in honour of their leader.

The leader himself strode across the room, brushing past people, heading in a straight line for Cassie's mother. To my astonishment, Cassie stepped forward to bar his way.

He stopped – he had to or he would have knocked her over – and looked down at her.

'Ah, the little Cassandra! How delightful!'

His voice was deep and rumbling with a vaguely central-European accent. He bent and kissed Cassie's hand with a flourish.

Now I knew I hated him.

Pulling her hand back, Cassie said, 'Hello, Mr Lukas. I'd like to introduce Ben Harker, a friend of mine.'

'How do you do, young fellow?' boomed Lukas. He held out his hand and attempted to deliver a bone-crushing handshake. I foiled him by letting my own hand go limp. With a contemptuous smile, he dropped my hand and bowed to Cassie.

'Now I must pay my respects to your charming mother.'

He resumed his interrupted journey across the room, followed by his three faithful companions.

Cassie and I watched him barge into Mrs Sinclair's group and monopolise her attention. She didn't seem to mind. He chatted away in his deep, mellow voice. His three followers took up strategic positions close by, gazing suspiciously about the room.

Somehow I could sense from Cassie that the big man, Lukas, was the reason I was here.

'What do you make of him?' asked Cassie.

'Apart from the fact that he's too big, too good-looking and oozing with phony continental charm, I suppose he's harmless.'

'He isn't,' said Cassie quietly. 'He's evil. He and Mum are mixed up in some kind of big business deal. Unless she breaks away from him, he'll destroy her.'

Chapter Three

Investigation

The intensity in Cassie's voice had attracted the barman's attention, and he gave us a curious glance. We moved further away from the bar.

'Is there a quiet corner where we can talk?' I asked.

Cassie looked round. 'There's the balcony.'

We drifted across the room to a glass door on the left-hand side. It led out on to a sizeable balcony with a scattering of café-type tables and chairs. We moved to a table at the far end and sat down.

'This feeling you have about Lukas,' I said. 'This is one of your –'

'One of my crazy ideas,' said Cassie defiantly.

'I wasn't going to say that,' I said soothingly. 'Since

that coach crash I take your – *ideas* very seriously.' I paused. 'I don't really understand how this second sight business works.'

'I don't understand it myself,' said Cassie miserably. 'Sometimes it's objects, things. As soon as I touched the door I knew that coach was going to crash. Sometimes it's dreams, but they're usually horribly muddled.'

'And sometimes it's people?'

She nodded. 'I seem to be able to sense things about people. If they're lying, if they've got some kind of secret plan, if they're not really the way they pretend to be.'

'And you got some sort of feeling about Lukas?'

'It was different with him,' said Cassie. 'Stronger than ever before.'

'And what did you see, or sense or whatever?'

'Evil,' said Cassie quietly. 'Evil and death.'

'That's pretty powerful stuff.'

'He's surrounded by it,' said Cassie. 'It hovers over him like a cloud. I can almost see it.'

'Where does he actually come from?'

'He says he's Hungarian by birth. He says his family were refugees, persecuted by the Communists. He's lived and worked all over Europe.'

'He must have lived through some pretty violent

events,' I said. 'Maybe that's left its mark on him.'

'I'm sure he has,' said Cassie. 'But it's not just that. He's actually killed people, I know he has, more than once. He's quite prepared to kill again. That's why I'm so afraid.'

I did my best to reassure her. 'If he's fixing up some big business deal with your mother, he needs her help, her contacts. He's not likely to harm her.'

'Not on purpose, perhaps. But bad things happen around him, I know they do. And if Mum's involved . . .'

'Have you told your mother how you feel about him?'

Cassie sighed. 'I tried. But – well, you saw what she's like. She won't hear a word against him. She said she's checked all his references and his business credentials are impeccable. But I don't think it's just that . . .'

'You reckon she's fallen for that old continental charm?'

'He's got plenty of charm,' said Cassie angrily. 'But it's the devil's charm, I know it is. He's evil.'

I sat quietly for a moment, looking at the City streets spread out down below. It was the start of the weekend, and they were already beginning to empty.

'I'm sorry,' said Cassie after a moment. 'I should never have involved you in all this, it isn't your problem.'

'Don't be daft,' I said. 'It's our problem. We're a team, aren't we? I was just thinking about what to do next.'

'And?' said Cassie hopefully.

'It's not like the problem with the school coach,' I said slowly.

'How do you mean?'

'You knew the coach was going to crash, right?'

'Right.'

'But not for a reason that anyone was likely to believe. The answer there was to get you off the coach – and for me to pass on a warning in a way people could accept.'

'But Mum won't get off the coach,' said Cassie 'And we can't just wait around and see what happens.'

'And there's no way she'll accept a warning based simply on your instincts?'

Cassie shook her head. 'No chance. I've already tried. Mum's a lawyer. She doesn't believe in instincts, she believes in evidence.'

'Then we must find her some,' I said.

Cassie looked baffled. 'How?'

'By checking up on Lukas, investigating him.'

'There won't be anything to find.'

'What makes you so sure?'

'Because Mum's no fool. As I said, she checked him

out before doing business with him. If she'd found anything suspicious . . .'

'Ah, but we've got one big advantage,' I said.

'What's that?'

'We already know he's a villain. Now all we have to do is prove it.' For some reason I was quite sure that Cassie was right about Lukas.

'All right,' said Cassie. 'Where do we start?'

'I'm not sure yet,' I admitted. 'But I'll think of something.'

'Yes,' said Cassie. 'You will.' She stood up. 'We ought to go back inside.'

'Can't we get out of here? Let's go out for that pizza. I hate things on sticks and I don't think I can stand much more of this.'

'I'll have to go and ask Mum.'

'Tell,' I said.

'What?'

'Don't ask her, tell her. Never ask permission when the answer might be no. Just say, "Ben and I are going out for a pizza," and smile politely as if it was all settled. Got it?'

'Right.' She grinned happily at me and my heart – well, you know that bit.

We went back inside. Nothing seemed to have changed; the party was still in full swing.

I looked round. 'This lot will be here all night.'

Cassie shook her head. 'Mum will have them out of here inside an hour.'

'How will she manage that?'

'By telling the caterers to cut off the drink supply. You'd be amazed how quickly they all disappear!'

We made our way over to her mother, who was still deep in conversation with Lukas.

'Excuse me,' said Cassie with a dazzling smile. 'Ben and I are just going out for a pizza.'

She was a quick learner. It worked like a charm.

'All right, dear,' said her mother vaguely. 'Don't be too late. Don't forget you're going to Cambridge to see your father tomorrow; you'll want to make an early start.'

Then Lukas chimed in. 'Ah, the two young people together,' he rumbled, giving us a patronising smile. 'How delightful!'

At which point my big mouth took over again.

'I hear you're from Hungary,' I said.

'That is so, young fellow. You know my country?'

'No, but I had a Hungarian friend at my last school. He told me lots of proverbs about Hungarians.'

'Proverbs?' said Lukas. He gave me a sinister smile, and I wished I'd never started this.

'Old sayings,' I said. 'Like, "A Hungarian is someone

who follows you into a revolving door and comes out in front of you." Or, "When you shake hands with a Hungarian, count your fingers afterwards."' I smiled at Cassie's mother. 'I'd be careful doing business with this man if I were you!'

Lukas threw back his head and gave a booming laugh. But he wasn't really amused.

'It is true, there are many such sayings.' He dropped a massive hand on my shoulder, catching it in a painful grip. 'Here is another one for you. "With a Hungarian for a friend, you don't need enemies!" Perhaps you remember that – my friend?'

I managed to free my shoulder. 'I certainly will!'

I was pretty angry by now, and I made what turned out to be one smart remark too many.

'We must talk again, Mr Lukas. I'd love to know more about your fascinating Hungarian business deals.'

'I do not discuss my affairs with children,' said Lukas dismissively.

'No? Then I must see what I can find out on my own.'

I regretted the words as soon as they were out of my mouth.

Lukas gave me a menacing smile. 'That would be – unwise.'

I saw Mrs Sinclair giving Lukas a worried look.

She was obviously puzzled by the exchange, and by Lukas's angry tone.

Cassie grabbed my hand and tugged me towards the door.

'Goodnight, Mrs Sinclair,' I said. 'Thanks for a most interesting evening.'

We made our escape.

Going down in the lift, Cassie said disapprovingly, 'That was subtle. First you insult him and then you threaten him!'

'Well, he made me angry.'

'So I gathered. You're not nearly as mild-mannered as you look, are you? And why all the slurs about Hungarians?'

'No such thing,' I protested. 'I really did have a Hungarian friend at my last school. He taught me all those proverbs. Real Hungarians are proud of their devious reputation! Lukas annoyed me, so I wanted to annoy him back.'

'You certainly managed that!'

I rubbed my still-aching shoulder. 'You're telling me! Still it wasn't entirely a waste of time. I think we put a few doubts in your mother's mind. She gave him a distinctly funny look when he turned ugly.'

We came out of the lift, crossed the foyer, and made

our way to the garden café. It was getting a bit cool to sit outside, so we found a booth and ordered our pizzas. It was bright and cheerful – red and white checked tablecloths, candles in straw-covered Chianti bottles and a friendly Italian waitress.

'As a matter of fact,' I went on, 'I don't think Lukas is really Hungarian anyway.'

Cassie looked puzzled. 'Why ever not?'

'I told you, I had this Hungarian friend, so I got to know the accent pretty well. Lukas doesn't sound quite right.'

'So what is he, then, if he's not Hungarian?'

'I think he's Russian,' I said. 'But why is he lying about it?'

'Because he's evil,' said Cassie. 'So what do we do next?'

'Like I said, we check up on Lukas. It's a pity Dad's away this week, he'd be able to help. But I do have some other contacts.'

Cassie gave a determined nod. 'We'll start tomorrow.'

I laughed. 'We'll start on Monday. It's the weekend, nothing happens in the City over the weekend. But we've got all next week. It's half-term, remember?'

'All the same, we'll start tomorrow,' said Cassie determinedly. 'I'm due to go up to Cambridge to see my father.'

‘Do you think he’ll be able to help?’

‘He’s a professor of law, he ought to know something about crime.’

‘I thought you said he specialised in medieval law.’

‘So he does. But even if he can’t help us himself, he might know someone who can.’

‘Networking!’ I said. ‘Your mother would be proud.’

‘We can go up tomorrow, make a day of it,’ said Cassie. Suddenly she looked stricken. ‘Unless you’ve got something else to do?’

I mentally reviewed my arrangements for Saturday: morning coffee with a French girl called Yvonne, with whom I was developing a promising relationship. A kickabout in the park in the afternoon with some friends from class. A computer war-games session with my mate John later on Saturday afternoon. We were re-fighting the battle of Gettysburg, and I was winning. A night out with a gang of mates at a new club, the Purple Pineapple.

I weighed them in the balance against a day out with Cassie in Cambridge and cheerfully blew out the lot of them.

‘Not a thing,’ I said. ‘Cambridge it is!’

‘Good,’ said Cassie. ‘I’ll meet you outside tomorrow morning.’

Our pizzas arrived and we settled down to eat.

Personally, I didn't think talking to a few doddering old professors would do us much good. Still, Cassie was keen and at least it would be safe.

As it happened, I couldn't have been more wrong.

Chapter Four

Dangerous Journey

I'd assumed we'd be making the trip to Cambridge by train, but when I arrived in the main forecourt next morning to meet Cassie as arranged, I found her sitting in the back of a chauffeur-driven limousine. She opened the door and waved me over.

'What's all this?' I asked.

'Mum sends me up by car if she's not coming herself. She doesn't like me going by train alone.'

She moved over and I got in beside her.

'Well, you're not alone, are you?'

'By the time I told her you were coming the car was already ordered. There didn't seem any point in cancelling it. You don't mind, do you?'

I sank back in the luxurious leather seat as the car moved smoothly away. 'I think I can bear it.'

'I wonder if Daddy will be able to help us,' said Cassie. The frown was back, and I could tell she was still worrying about her mother. 'I called last night and told him a bit about the problem.'

I put a finger to my lips and nodded towards the driver's back. He was on the other side of the glass screen, but that was no guarantee he couldn't hear us.

Cassie looked puzzled for a moment and then nodded.

I didn't have any real reason to distrust the chauffeur, but I felt the less said about Lukas the better.

'I'm sure your father will be very helpful,' I went on. 'He can tell us the best places to visit and bring us up to date on the latest in medieval law.'

We spent the rest of the journey talking about everyday things – like school.

'I'm a bit worried about going back after half-term,' said Cassie.

'What for?' I asked.

'All that fuss I made about the coach trip.'

'Don't worry,' I said. 'By the time we go back it'll all be forgotten.'

'I hope so,' said Cassie. 'I hate people looking sideways at me all the time, thinking I'm weird. No wonder the original Cassandra got so fed up.'

'What original Cassandra?'

'Daughter of a Greek king called Priam.'

'What happened to her?'

'The god Apollo made a pass at her and she turned him down. She got cursed with the gift of prophecy – only her prophecies were never believed.'

'How did you get the name, anyway?'

'Mum's got a name from the Greek Classics – Helen, as in Helen of Troy. And Daddy just liked the sound of Cassandra. I don't suppose he thought about the other associations.'

'What became of her in the end – the original Cassandra?'

Cassie shuddered. 'She got murdered.'

I patted her shoulder. 'Don't worry. As old Shakespeare said, "What's in a name?" '

'Altogether too much in my case! I sometimes wonder if I inherited the curse because of it.'

'I doubt it.' I thought for a moment. 'Do your parents know about all this spooky stuff? They must do, surely?'

'Dad's got a vague idea, but he doesn't really take it seriously.'

'And your mother?'

'She knows and she doesn't. She doesn't believe in that sort of thing so it can't be happening – even if it is!'

'Something to do with being a lawyer,' I said. 'They're trained to ignore inconvenient facts.'

Cassie sighed. 'The general family position is, I'm a bit neurotic and highly-strung, but I'll probably grow out of it.'

'Maybe you will. Perhaps it's something to do with adolescence – like spots.'

'Believe me, I'd sooner have spots!'

'Oh no you wouldn't. I had a terrible time when I was thirteen. Face like a pizza!'

It's not all that far to Cambridge, and the traffic was pretty light. In just over an hour and a half we were drawing up outside Cassie's father's college, the first one you came to as you drove into town.

We got out of the car and Cassie went up to the driver's window.

'We're going to have lunch with my father and then take a look around town. Could you pick us up back here at six o'clock, please?'

The chauffeur touched his uniform cap. 'Very good, miss. Six o'clock.' He drove away.

We walked through the main entrance, past the porter's lodge, and found ourselves facing an enormous lawn surrounded by elegant eighteenth century buildings.

I looked round. 'Very impressive!'

'This college is a bit of a newcomer in Cambridge terms,' said Cassie. 'It wasn't built until seventeen ninety-one.' She pointed to a distant corner, over on the left. 'Daddy's rooms are over there.'

'Right,' I said, and set off across the lawn.

Cassie grabbed my arm and hauled me back on to the path. 'Not over the lawn!'

'Why not? It's the quickest way.'

'It's not allowed, that's why not.'

I pointed to a tall figure in a black gown strolling across the lawn on the other side. 'He's walking on it, why can't we?'

'Because he's a don,' said Cassie severely. 'We're not even in the university. Come on, this way.'

We followed the path round the edge of the lawn and eventually reached the corner she'd indicated. We found ourselves outside an arched doorway, beyond which was a steep stone staircase. A list of names was painted on the side of the arch. The name at the top of the list was Professor J. Sinclair.

We climbed to the top of the staircase and came to a set of closed oak doors.

Cassie looked at them in dismay. 'He's sporting his oak!'

'Come again?'

'Rooms in college have two sets of doors. If the outer ones, the oak ones, are shut, it's called "sporting your oak". That means either you're out, or you're in but you don't want to be disturbed.'

'Look, your father is expecting you, isn't he?'

'Well, yes, but he's very absent-minded. And if someone's sporting their oak you're supposed to go quietly away.'

'That's even dafter than not walking on the lawn,' I said.

I hammered on the door with my fist.

After a few minutes of determined banging, the door opened and a cross-looking man appeared. He was small and thin with close-cropped brown hair and a short, neatly trimmed brown beard. Both hair and beard were bristling with fury.

'What the devil do you think –' He broke off as he saw Cassie behind me. 'Oh dear, oh dear!'

Cassie gave him a reproachful look. 'Daddy, you forgot!'

'Well, not forgot exactly, I was a little preoccupied. Come in, come in!'

'This is my friend Ben,' said Cassie.

Professor Sinclair grabbed my hand, pumped it vigorously, and ushered us both into the room.

It was a big, comfortably-furnished, old-fashioned

room with a high ceiling and small arched windows. It seemed to be a combination sitting-room, dining-room and study. The walls were lined with books, and more books were piled up on chairs and on the floor.

A table under the window was set with lunch for four. There was a bottle of wine in an ice-bucket and a jug of beer and another jug of what looked like lemonade.

'I didn't forget entirely,' said the professor. 'I got a cold collation sent up from the buttery. Then I got absorbed in some work . . .' He swept a pile of books and papers from the end of the table, dumping them on to a chair.

'A glass of wine, young man? Or some of the college ale?' He looked at me again. 'Perhaps not. Cassie always drinks lemonade.'

'Lemonade will be fine, sir.'

He poured glasses of lemonade for us both and a glass of white wine for himself, talking all the time.

'Cassie phoned last night and said you wanted advice on some more contemporary aspect of the law. I've asked Jim Broadbent to join us. He specialises in something called Criminal Economics, one of these new subjects.'

Jim Broadbent turned up a few minutes later, a tubby young man in a baggy tweed suit. He accepted a tankard of college ale and we sat down to lunch.

It was an excellent lunch: cold ham, cold beef, cold salmon, a variety of green salads. The lemonade was delicious, and the professor and Jim seemed very happy with the ale and the wine.

When lunch was over, Jim said, 'So what seems to be the problem?'

Cassie looked appealingly at me and I said, 'It's a bit vague, I'm afraid. Cassie's mum is mixed up in a deal with a financial entrepreneur called Lukas. He claims to be Hungarian, although we think he may be Russian. Cassie's convinced he's untrustworthy. We thought it might help if we found out something about the general background. Anything at all you can tell us about foreign criminals and high finance.'

Jim emptied his tankard, sat back and delivered a brief but fascinating lecture on international crime and high finance. He said the big international criminal combines were making so much money, mostly from drugs, that they hardly knew what to do with it.

'They're cooperating more and more these days,' he said. 'The Italian and Sicilian Mafia, the Chinese Triads. The profits from crime in one country are hidden in another. Hidden and cleaned up, disguised as legitimate investments. They call it money-laundering.'

'What about Russia?' I asked.

'Russia's the worst of the lot. Completely chaotic.

When communism finally collapsed, the crooks took over. They've got links with the government and the *apparatchiks*, the civil service. These days criminal gangs are coming out into the open as political parties. Some of them even own their own banks!'

'How important is the Russian Mafia?'

'That's part of the problem. There isn't one, not really. Not in the same way there's an Italian one. Come to that, the Italian Mafia isn't as united as everyone thinks.'

'How do you mean?'

'Well, it's not just one big organisation, it's an association of associations. The different Families. Sometimes they quarrel, but mostly they cooperate, get on.'

'And the Russians?'

'Just a collection of squabbling rival gangs. You never know what they'll do next. They're as likely to shoot each other as they are to cooperate.'

I thought of what Cassie had said, about the aura of death that seemed to surround Lukas.

Cassie had been listening to all this, silent and wide-eyed, as if what Jim was saying confirmed all her worst fears.

'Surely these villains are not allowed to operate in England with impunity?' demanded Professor Sinclair. 'There must be security checks, that sort of thing?'

'To be sure,' agreed Jim. 'But checks can be evaded,

documents forged. And when someone seems to have access to unlimited amounts of money, people don't always ask as many questions as they should.'

We talked a little longer but there wasn't much more he could tell us. He'd never heard of Lukas though, as he said, that probably wasn't the man's real name anyway. He promised to make enquiries.

'Trouble is, I'm a bit out of touch up here. If this Lukas is a new player, you really want someone on the ground. They've got a pretty good gossip grapevine in the City. Someone's bound to know something about him.'

I stood up. 'I think I may know just the someone. I'll get in touch with him on Monday.' I caught Cassie's eye and she turned to her father.

'We'd better let you get back to your work, Daddy. Ben and I want to take a look around Cambridge.'

The professor protested for a bit to be polite, but we could see he didn't really mind. As a family man, he was pretty detached.

'Don't worry too much about your mother, my dear,' he told Cassie. 'She's very shrewd, and I'm sure she won't do anything silly.'

The professor, I thought, wasn't quite living in the real world. And he'd never met Lukas . . .

We said goodbye to Professor Sinclair and to Jim

Broadbent, and went down the staircase, along the path and out of the college.

We had a nice afternoon wandering around Cambridge. Cassie showed me several ancient colleges – really ancient ones, not eighteenth century newcomers like her father's one. Since it was a sunny afternoon, we went down to the river and hired a punt.

To be honest, I was more than a bit worried about this. I'd never punted before, and I had visions of clinging, monkey-like, to the pole while the boat floated from underneath me.

I needn't have bothered. Cassie insisted on doing the punting herself, showing an amazing mastery of the long pole. She'd learned the art on previous visits to Cambridge to see her father.

'The trick is not to shove the pole in too hard or it gets stuck,' she said. 'You trail it behind you in between shoves, using it as a rudder.'

So I lay back on the punt cushions, letting Cassie do all the work. Sometimes I think there's a lot to be said for Women's Lib.

We got back a bit late to the boat-hire place, and we had to rush back to the college to meet our car by six o'clock. We were about ten minutes late.

The car was waiting outside the college gate and, as

we ran up, the driver reached back through his window and opened the passenger door for us.

We jumped inside, slamming the door, and the car zoomed away.

We collapsed back in the seat, tired and happy.

At least that's how we started off. We were talking over the events of the day when Cassie went suddenly quiet. She grabbed my arm painfully hard, and her eyes went wide and staring.

'What is it?' I asked. 'What's the matter, Cassie?'

'Danger,' she whispered. 'We're in danger.'

I could actually feel the anxiety radiating off of her.

'What sort of danger?'

'I don't know. Somehow things just aren't right.'

I looked round the car. Everything seemed to be all right. Then I looked out of the back window and saw the black car following us.

It was one of those expensive foreign jobs, a Mercedes or a BMW. It had darkened windows so you couldn't see inside the car. It made the car look sinister, like someone wearing dark glasses.

The car was gaining on us rapidly, as if determined to pass us. But we were in a narrow, winding lane, and there was no room to pass.

'Danger,' whispered Cassie. 'Terrible danger.'

The big black car sped closer . . .

Chapter Five

Escape

I forced myself to be calm and sat back in my seat, thinking hard.

I turned to Cassie. 'Seat belts, quick,' I said.

Like too many people in the back seats of cars, we hadn't got round to putting them on. It never seems as urgent as it does when you're riding in the front seat.

We strapped on our seat belts and looked out of the back window again.

The big black car was right behind us now, almost on the rear bumper.

I opened the partition and spoke to the chauffeur. 'We seem to have some kind of maniac on our tail.'

'I know, sir, I've had him in my rear-view mirror for quite a while. Amazing how many idiots there are behind the wheels of expensive cars.'

'This one seems worse than most,' I said. 'It almost looks as if he's out to get us. Be careful, won't you?'

It wasn't much of a warning but it was all I could think of.

The driver laughed. 'Don't worry, there's nothing much he can do on a road like this. There's a stretch of dual carriageway ahead. He'll be able to pass then, and we'll be rid of him.'

But the driver of the big black car didn't wait for the dual carriageway. On the next bend he zoomed up beside us, forcing us clean off the road.

We went straight through a hedge, lurched across a field, scattering cattle, and crashed into a tree.

There was a screech of rending metal and the car rolled on to its side. Only our seat belts prevented us from ending up in a tangle on the floor.

'You all right?' I asked, moving gingerly.

'I think so.'

Through the cracked partition we could see the driver, lying unconscious over the steering wheel.

Cassie undid her seat belt and scrambled upright. She turned to me, wild-eyed. 'That driver deliberately made us crash the car. We could all have been killed!'

'The odds were against it,' I said. 'The car wasn't moving that fast, not in a narrow, winding lane. Anyway, we're still alive. Now, if we can only get out of this car . . .'

I tried the door on my side, which was now above us. It seemed to have jammed in the crash.

'Come on, Cassie,' I said. 'Let's try and kick it open.'

We wriggled round and both started kicking up at the door. At the third attempt it sprang open and we climbed out into the field.

As we got out, the driver moaned and stirred. By the time we got round to the front of the car he'd recovered consciousness. We helped him out of the driver's door.

'Are you all right?' I asked.

He rubbed a bruise on his forehead. 'I think so. You saw, it wasn't my fault. That driver was a lunatic, forced me right off the road.'

'Don't worry,' said Cassie soothingly. 'Nobody's going to blame you. Any chance of pushing the car over and getting out of this field?'

The driver studied the damage. The front of the car had been crumpled by the tree.

He shook his head. 'Tow job, I'm afraid. I can call for help on the radio – if it's still working. Otherwise I'll have to find a phone.'

'If you're sure you're all right, we'll have to get back,' I said. 'We'll call for help as well at the first phone we come to.'

The black car had disappeared down the road by now, but I didn't fancy staying with the wreck in case it came back. I felt bad about leaving the chauffeur, but I didn't think our unknown enemy had anything against him. I wanted to get Cassie away from there as soon as possible.

Assuring the driver once again that it wasn't his fault, we set off.

We left the field through the gap in the hedge made by our sudden arrival and headed back down the lane the way we'd come.

'Now what?' asked Cassie as we tramped along between the hedgerows.

'We'll just have to get back to London the best way we can.'

'Shouldn't we call my mother? And the police?'

'Calling your mother would only upset and worry her. We should call the police and report the accident, I suppose. Let's just concentrate on getting ourselves home, and then think about what to do next.'

As it happened, our luck was in. We managed to hitch a lift to the nearest village from a passing farm truck. I called the police from the local post office and reported seeing a crashed car in a field outside the village. When they asked for my name, I put down the phone.

We got a bus from there into Cambridge, and from Cambridge we caught the next train back to London. I'd brought plenty of cash with me – Dad gives me a bigger allowance than I can spend. All the same, Cassie insisted on buying the tickets with her credit card.

In the taxi on the way back to Pennington Towers we discussed our next move. Cassie was all for telling her mother, but I managed to talk her out of it.

'You know what'll happen,' I said. 'She'll call in the police, and because she's a high-powered lawyer they'll take her seriously. My father will hear about it and he'll make a fuss as well.'

'What's wrong with that?'

'Don't you see? We've both got very successful – and very rich – parents. They may think it was an attempted kidnapping, for ransom. We'll be surrounded by policemen and bodyguards all day. We'll lose all our freedom.'

'Lukas was behind it, I'm sure of that,' said Cassie. 'But why? What was he trying to do?'

It was a very good question.

'Scare us off,' I said. 'He must have sensed we were some kind of danger to him. It's my fault, I'm afraid.

I obviously went too far yesterday at your mother's party.'

'Well if he thinks he can scare me off, he's got another thing coming,' said Cassie.

It struck me again that she was a lot tougher than she looked. If we were going to carry on investigating Lukas, she'd need to be.

'All right, then,' she said. 'So what do we do now?'

'Nothing – for the moment. We'll lay low tonight and tomorrow, and start again on Monday. Dad will still be away, but I've got a contact in the City who may be able to help us. He was head boy at my last school.'

'What do we say to my mother?'

'Just tell her what a nice day we had visiting your father.'

Cassie looked puzzled. 'But why hush everything up?'

'Three reasons. It avoids worrying your mother. It stops us finding ourselves knee-deep in bodyguards. Most important of all, it will puzzle Lukas.'

Cassie got the point straight away. 'He'll be expecting us to turn up all terrified, yelling and screaming about being in an accident. So if we just ignore the whole thing . . .'

'He'll wonder what we're up to,' I said. 'With any luck, it will put him off-balance.'

So that's what we decided to do. I still say it was a pretty good plan. Only things didn't quite work out like that.

I paid off the taxi outside Pennington Towers and saw Cassie up to her mother's flat. Cassie led me into her mother's study where we found her at her desk, eating sandwiches, drinking coffee and working her way through a pile of legal papers.

Cassie didn't seem a bit surprised, and I realised it must be like this most evenings. Poor Cassie, I thought, an absentee father, a workaholic mother and an unwanted gift of second sight. No wonder she was highly strung.

Then I thought that her situation wasn't so very different from my own. Except in my case it was an absentee mother and a workaholic father – and no second sight to worry about.

Cassie's mother looked up from her work. 'Hello, love. Hello, Ben. You're late.'

'It was such a lovely day,' said Cassie. 'And we went on the river.'

You'll notice both those statements were completely true. Yet somehow they suggested an answer to the question without actually giving one. Cassie might not have my vivid imagination but she wasn't doing badly.

Anyway, Cassie's mother accepted the answer without comment.

'Is Ben staying for supper?' she asked.

Cassie grinned. 'If there is any.'

Her mother looked guilty. 'I sent out for some sandwiches. Do you think you could manage to rustle up some supper for the pair of you? There's lots of stuff in the kitchen. Or you can send out for pizza or Chinese if you like.' She glanced at me and smiled. 'I'm afraid we only get staff in for the formal occasions. The rest of the time we exist on tinned food, TV dinners and takeaways.'

'Lifestyles of the rich and famous,' I said. 'Dad and me are much the same. If Dad isn't at a business banquet he lives on beans on toast.'

'I'll see what we can find,' said Cassie. 'Coming, Ben?'

I nodded. 'I'll even help. I can boil a kettle if someone points me in the right direction.'

Cassie's mother was already absorbed in her work, and I followed Cassie out of the room, along the hall and into a large, super-modern, stainless-steel kitchen.

Cassie looked round a little helplessly. I suspected that, like her mother, she wasn't really the domestic type.

'I could try to cook something – or shall we just send out?'

'Got any pasta?' I asked.

'I think so.'

'Mince? Onions? Tinned tomatoes? Garlic? I do a smashing spag bol!'

'What?'

'*Spaghetti bolognese*. Or I could do *carbonara* if you've got any bacon.'

She stared at me in astonishment. 'You don't mean to say you can really cook?'

'Up to a point,' I said modestly. 'Our housekeeper's not much of a cook. I got tired of either eating out or ordering in takeaways, so I learned a few of the basics.'

I started rooting through the cupboards, assembling the ingredients.

'Is there anything I can do to help?'

'Sure there is. Get a very large pan, fill it with water and bring it to the boil. Sprinkle a little salt in.'

'That I can manage.'

She put the water on to boil and I got on with chopping up the ingredients.

We were waiting for the water to boil when the phone rang.

Cassie picked it up. 'Yes? Yes, I see. I'll tell her. Thank you.'

Her voice was calm as she put the phone down, but there was panic in her eyes.

'That was main reception. Lukas is on his way up.'

They'd let him up because he was a frequent visitor. But they'd rung up so Cassie's mum could be out if she wanted.

Cassie said, 'I'd better go and tell Mum. What are we going to say?'

I was thinking hard. 'Nothing. Let him do the talking. Don't warn your mother and don't go and answer the door either. Let her go.'

We waited in tense silence.

A few minutes later we heard the sighing of the lift. Moments later there was an urgent ringing of the bell.

We heard Cassie's mother's voice from the study. 'Can you get that, Cassie?'

I put a hand on Cassie's arm and shook my head.

The bell rang again, louder and more urgently.

We heard Mrs Sinclair come out of the study muttering, 'Who the devil . . . ?'

We heard her go down the corridor and open the front door.

'Lukas! What a surprise!'

Then Lukas's deep rumbling tones. 'My poor Helen! You must be shattered! If there is anything, anything I can do!'

'Lukas, what are you talking about?' She sounded more irritated than alarmed.

Lukas, on the other hand, sounded amazed. 'You haven't heard? No one has contacted you?'

'I haven't heard anything from anyone. What's all this about?' Before Lukas could reply she went on, 'Don't stand there in the hall, you'd better come in. I'm in the study.'

We heard the front door close and two sets of footsteps, one light, one heavy, going along the corridor towards the study.

Cassie and I slipped out of the kitchen and tiptoed after them.

Through the open door we saw Lukas and Mrs Sinclair, facing each other in the centre of the room, Lukas with his back to the door.

'But the children,' Lukas was saying. 'There was an accident. Something happened to the car. They may have been hurt. You must let me help you.'

'Rubbish!' said Helen Sinclair. 'Where did you hear this ridiculous story?'

Before Lukas could reply, I stepped through the open doorway, Cassie close behind me.

'Yes, Mr Lukas,' I said. 'Where *did* you hear the story? Exactly what made you think that we'd been in an accident?'

Chapter Six

Stand-off

Though I say it myself, it was a great moment. Lukas spun round and saw us standing in the doorway.

He looked utterly astonished – in fact the word 'gobsmacked' comes irresistibly to mind.

I suppose it was understandable. The driver of the black car must have reported successfully causing the car crash. Lukas would have assumed we'd been hurt in the accident. At the the very least he expected us to be frightened, shaken and bruised. Instead, here we were, safe and sound at home, acting as if nothing had happened.

Mrs Sinclair was looking at him with a thoughtful

expression on her face. That alone made it all worthwhile. If we could plant a few doubts about Lukas in her mind, we'd have gone some way towards blocking his evil schemes – whatever they were.

Apart from the accident I still only had the evidence of Cassie's strange instinct that he had any evil schemes. At the same time, I realised that I had no doubts at all about her being right. It was a tribute to the link that had grown between us.

'Well,' said Mrs Sinclair sharply. 'Where did you hear this ridiculous tale?'

Just for a moment, Lukas was totally flustered. 'I'm not sure. I think I saw it on the news.'

Mrs Sinclair shook her head. 'I watched the early evening news before I sat down to work. There was nothing then.'

'Then someone must have told me,' said Lukas, recovering his cool. 'A phone call, some scrap of gossip.'

'Strange though, all the same, isn't it?' I said. 'I mean, how could a ridiculous rumour like that get about?'

'And how would it reach you?' asked Cassie innocently. 'Quite a mystery, isn't it?'

Lukas shot me a look of pure hatred that chilled my blood. I suddenly realised what a dangerous enemy I had made. He'd been quite prepared to fix up a car crash just because he thought I might get underfoot in some way, but now I had jeopardised his business relationship with Cassie's mother. Worse still, I'd made a fool of him. Now it was personal.

I'd put myself and Cassie in terrible danger. Something had to be done. I began thinking furiously.

While I was thinking, Lukas managed to come up with a plausible story. 'It was the radio!' he said suddenly. 'I was listening to the radio in my car. One of the news stations, I can't remember which one. I heard that the daughter of someone important had been in a car crash in Cambridge and I jumped to the wrong conclusion.'

I gave him a sceptical look. 'Pretty strange coincidence, all the same.'

'Yes indeed,' said Lukas stiffly. 'The whole business is something of a mystery. I am happy to be proven wrong.' He turned and bowed to Cassie's mother. 'I can only apologise for disturbing you, and for alarming you unnecessarily. I look forward to our meeting on Monday. Matters are reaching a crucial stage. Goodnight!'

He turned and marched from the room. Cassie's mother moved automatically to see him out. 'Let me do it,' I said, and hurried after him.

I caught him at the door.

'Just as well really, isn't it, Mr Lukas?' I said politely.

He glared down at me. 'What?'

'That the story you heard was untrue and we hadn't been in a car crash.'

'Just as well for you,' he said grimly.

'And for you,' I said.

'What do you mean?'

'I gather you're involved in some big business deal with Cassie's mother – the one that's reaching a crucial stage.'

'That does not concern you.'

'It concerns Cassie,' I said. 'If anything happened to her, like being hurt in a car crash, her mother would be quite distracted. She'd be too upset to concentrate on business.'

'And if something unfortunate happened to you?'

'Same difference. I'm Cassie's friend. Cassie would be very upset – and if Cassie's upset, her mother's upset too.'

He nodded. 'Then you'd better take care, young man. Don't do anything that might get you hurt.'

'Oh, I won't,' I said. 'Believe me, I don't want any trouble.'

He marched out. Thankfully, I closed the door behind him. Perhaps I'd managed to buy a little time, achieved a temporary stand-off. I hoped I'd sold him the idea that if he left us alone, we'd leave him alone.

Actually I'd no intention of giving up on checking him out. But if he thought we'd been scared off, he might leave us alone for a while.

Long enough for us to get the goods on him . . .

I heard the phone ring as I went along the corridor. When I got back to the study I found Mrs Sinclair was talking to someone.

'Yes, I see,' she was saying. 'Yes it's all very puzzling. But I assure you they're both here, safe and sound. I'll talk to them and call you back if they can be of any help.'

She slammed down the phone and turned to face us, a steely gleam in her eye. All at once she was the top lawyer, cross-examining a dodgy witness.

'Now, perhaps you two will tell me what really happened? That was the car-hire company. They say their driver had an accident, went off the road. They wanted to be sure you'd got back safely.' She turned to Cassie. 'Well, young lady?'

Cassie surprised me by rising to the occasion like a champ. 'We didn't want to worry you,' she said calmly. 'It was a minor accident and nobody was hurt. There didn't seem to be any point in upsetting you.'

I think Mrs Sinclair had her doubts, but she decided to buy the story, at least for the time being.

'I think I'll let the hire car company sort it out. We'll use another firm next time.'

I decided to get out while I was ahead.

'Well, we must let you get back to your work – and we must get back to our spaghetti.'

Back in the kitchen our pan of water had almost boiled dry, so Cassie filled it up again and I started on the sauce.

'Well done, Cassie,' I said. 'A really good story, and some of it was even true.'

Cassie looked pleased and guilty at the same time. 'I seem to be picking up some of your techniques. I still think we should have told her the whole story, though.'

I shook my head. 'Too soon. If she knew the whole truth she'd panic and call the police. We'll tell her when we've got more of a story to tell. More evidence.'

And there we left it.

Needless to say my spag bol was a triumph. We finished it off, then watched a bit of telly in Cassie's little sitting-room. We arranged to meet next day and I went off to my own flat in the North Tower.

It felt curiously empty – which of course it was, since the housekeeper had gone to bed and Dad was still away. It was something I'd never really noticed before. I'm used to being on my own and usually I quite like it. I realised how quickly I'd got used to having Cassie around, how important it had become to see her all the time. Maybe it was because of all we had in common. We were both only children, both loners. Maybe it was because of the way we seemed to understand each other without using words.

Mostly it was because she was so beautiful, and so much fun to be with.

And because she seemed to need me.

I started thinking about Cassie's odd gift – or curse – of second sight, and how readily I'd accepted it. I'd had a certain amount of proof, of course. The school coach crash, and her sudden sense of danger in the car. And her feelings about Lukas.

I realised I didn't know much about the paranormal. Perhaps I'd find it easier to watch out for Cassie if I knew a bit more. So I did what I always do when I feel short of vital information. I went to my study and logged on to the Internet.

Inevitably, there was an incredible number of sites dealing with the paranormal in one way or another.

I learned about UFO sightings, alien landings at Roswell, poltergeists and psychics and hauntings of every kind. Finally I found the site I was looking for, one specifically devoted to paranormal powers – telepathy, telekinesis, divination and second sight.

I discovered that my crack about Cassie's powers being a teenage thing like acne hadn't been so far out.

Just about the most common ghostly phenomenon there is is the poltergeist – German for 'noisy ghost'. Poltergeists slam doors in the middle of the night, smash cups, send objects flying across the room.

Paranormal researchers have discovered that when poltergeists pop up there's always an unhappy teenager around, usually a girl. There was a well-documented case of a haunted office in Germany. Neon lights failed, light bulbs exploded, photocopiers leaked, file drawers opened and closed and mysterious rappings came from the walls.

The phenomena all started with the arrival of one teenage girl. When she left, the hauntings stopped.

I wondered if the crockery started flying when Cassie got mad.

Powers like hers – prescience or flashes of the future, picking up psychic impressions from objects, places or people, are not uncommon. Sometimes they fade in later life, sometimes not.

I absorbed spooky information until I started to nod off, and then went to bed.

I slept uneasily, haunted by dreams of flying crockery and little green men landing in flying saucers.

I had no idea how useful my research would turn out to be in the days to come. Or how much trouble Cassie's strange powers were going to cause . . .

Chapter Seven

Trouble in the City

Next day, Sunday, was a day off. At least, it was for us. Cassie's mother stayed at home working, presumably on her big deal. Cassie and I met for lunch at the Italian café, went for a walk, watched a video and talked endlessly about everything under the sun. A nice quiet day. A perfect day, simply because I was with Cassie.

We even managed not to talk about Lukas, though I could tell from Cassie's occasional worried frown that he was still in her thoughts.

I wondered if we were in his.

On Monday we went on with our investigation, and the trouble really began.

As we rode the Underground the couple of stops to the City, I told Cassie all about Buster Brown, my man in the City.

'We met at that free school I told you about, the one I went to before St John's. Buster was there as well. He was head boy. He's older than I am – a big, tough, rugby-playing hearty. By then he'd been expelled from all the best public schools in the country. He's got a hundred per cent fail rate in every imaginable exam.'

'However did you become friends?' asked Cassie. 'He sounds absolutely unbearable!'

'He sounds unbearable but he isn't,' I said. 'In his own way, he's a very nice bloke.'

'How did he become something in the City?'

I grinned. 'Simple. Daddy owns the firm. Buster joined straight after school. The funny thing is, he turned out to have a real talent for finance. Old Buster doesn't understand much, but he does understand money. Must be in the genes. Anyway, I e-mailed him this morning and asked him for any info he can find about Lukas. We're going to meet in his office.'

We got off at Bank tube station and walked along narrow streets lined with tall glass buildings. Buster's was one of the tallest and glassiest. We gave our names to the receptionist in the foyer, and a glass lift whisked us up to Buster's office, which was large and luxurious with a view over the City.

The moment I saw Buster, I burst out laughing. He'd transformed himself into the complete financial whizz kid: bow tie, red braces and all, but his bright blue eyes were as sparkling as ever, and his straw-coloured hair was all over the place as usual.

'Ben!' he roared. 'How are you, you old villain?' He gave me a great bear-hug and Cassie a beaming smile when I introduced her.

It was hard not to like Buster.

The greetings over, Buster got straight down to business.

'Soon as I got your e-mail, I made a few enquiries about this Lukas outfit. Between you and me, they're a funny lot.'

I glanced at Cassie. 'Funny, how?'

'Seem to have unlimited capital – and they don't seem to care how they spend it. They'll invest in anything, buy anything. Sometimes some long shot will come in – they bought a few dodgy electronics companies and e-commerce outfits and one or two came up trumps. But very often they seem to sell for less than they paid.'

'Do they come out up or down overall?' asked Cassie. 'Do they make a profit?'

Buster scowled, tugging at his hair. 'Amazingly enough, they do, sweetie. Like I say, some pretty amazing long-shot investments have come up. All in all, I'd say they have to be well ahead in the long run. Funny thing is, they don't seem to care if their investments show a profit or not. The cash just keeps on flowing.'

'Anything else?' asked Cassie. 'Anything really fishy – criminal even?'

'There was one story . . .'

Cassie and I leaned forward.

Buster lowered his voice. 'Lukas's lot were very keen on a particular takeover. One of the big finance houses. Trouble was, the chairman of the finance house was dead against it.'

'And?'

'He had an accident at a crucial stage in the negotiations.'

'What kind of an accident?' asked Cassie.

'Somebody ran his car off the road. He was killed in the crash.'

Cassie and I looked at each other.

'Can you chase that story up for us?' I asked.

Buster shrugged. 'I can try. Doesn't seem likely Lukas's company would risk anything really dodgy, though. They've got too much to lose, they're really big players now. There's a rumour they're just about to pull off some colossal deal. Helen Sinclair's involved, so it's got to be big-time. Very high-powered lady, our Helen.'

'So I've heard,' said Cassie gravely.

I grinned. I'd told him her name when I introduced her, but it obviously hadn't registered. Apart from finance, not a lot registered with old Buster.

He promised he'd make some more enquiries for us, and said he'd ring me at the end of the day. Typically, he was willing to go to all this trouble without asking why we wanted to know.

As we went down in the lift, Cassie said severely, ' "Sweetie!" '

I grinned. 'It's the only language he speaks. You must admit, he gave us some very useful information. And I bet he finds out more. Do anything for a friend, old Buster.'

I couldn't think of any more investigating to do till I heard from Buster, so we decided to make a day of it.

We went for a ride on the London Eye. Cassie's mother had been sent a couple of VIP tickets.

Cassie took me for lunch in a weird Japanese place where you sat at a round counter and the food chugged by on a conveyor belt. You grabbed what you fancied as it went by, and they worked out the bill from the number and colour of the dishes in front of you. Cassie was crazy about the stuff. Personally, I felt it looked better than it tasted, and left you still feeling hungry.

We went to the Tate Modern and saw a lot of weird stuff that was either great art, total rubbish, or possibly both.

Finally we went for a walk along the Embankment, had a snack in a riverside café and then headed for home.

As we walked back towards Pennington Towers I said, 'I wonder what else old Buster will come up with for us.'

'He's come up with quite a lot already,' said Cassie grimly. 'I've been brooding over it all afternoon. Your friend Buster confirmed all my worst suspicions.'

'It was all a bit general,' I objected. 'All we really learned is that Lukas is a rash investor – and *maybe* had somebody bumped off who was in his way.' I paused. 'Using a very familiar technique, I must admit.'

'Yes, but why is he such a rash investor?' asked Cassie. 'He may be a criminal but he's not a fool.'

'All right, then, why?'

'Remember what Dad's colleague Jim Broadbent said, back in Cambridge, about money-laundering? Put that together with what Buster said – and there you are!'

'Where?'

Cassie gave me an impatient look. I was obviously being dim.

'Say Lukas uses his dodgy funds to buy a failing company for five million, then sells it for four?'

'Sounds like a bit of a disaster.'

'For anyone else, yes. But for Lukas it's a good deal. Now he's got four million pounds he can account for. Clean money – laundered money. He's lost a million, but he can afford to lose a million.'

I was beginning to see what Cassie was getting at.

'And he doesn't always lose,' I said thoughtfully. 'A lot of his risky investments make a profit – and that's clean money as well. Well done, Cassie, you've got it!'

Cassie nodded, sure that she was right.

'He can gamble wildly, just because he doesn't really care if he wins or loses. His whole investment strategy is a front for money-laundering.'

I patted her on the back. 'Your mother isn't the only financial genius in the family.'

Mention of her mother made Cassie look worried. 'I think we ought to go to her, warn her before she gets in too deep.'

'I think you're right. Let's go back to my place first,

and see if Buster's phoned. He may give us a bit more evidence to convince her.'

There was no message from Buster when we got back to my flat, so I called his office to see if he was still around.

I got a shocked-sounding secretary. 'Mr Brown isn't here, he's in hospital. He was attacked in the street this afternoon.'

I got the name of the hospital and the room number out of her, and slammed down the phone. Then I picked it up again and ordered a taxi.

I told Cassie what had happened and we headed for the door.

We found Buster sitting up in bed – in a private room, of course – eating grapes and swigging champagne. He had a black eye, a broken nose, a missing tooth and suspected mild concussion. They were keeping him in overnight just to check, but he hoped to go home tomorrow.

Being Buster, he was perfectly cheerful and made light of his injuries. 'Had worse in the average rugby scrum, old boy.'

'What happened?' I asked.

'I made a few calls about this Lukas cover for you. Got a lot of iffy reactions, but nothing solid. I fixed up a meeting with an insurance broker chap who might know something about that car accident. Wasn't far, so I walked there. On the way, three dodgy-looking types jumped me. I fought like a lion, but they got me in the end.'

'What did they look like?' I asked.

'Swarthy-looking types with moustaches. One big, one skinny, one small.'

I glanced quickly at Cassie and she nodded. Lukas's three thugs, the ones who'd been with him at Mrs Sinclair's cocktail party.

'Did they say anything?' asked Cassie.

'One of them did, the big one – he seemed to be the boss. He said, "Is not wise to ask questions!" Then he hit me with some sort of cosh and I passed out.'

'I knew it!' I groaned. 'Lukas! It's all our fault, Buster.'

He waved aside my apologies. 'What's a few cuts and bruises in a good cause!'

'For heavens sake, don't ask any more questions for us,' I said. 'I think you told us enough anyway.'

I explained Cassie's theory. Buster said it was plausible.

We thanked him again, said our goodbyes and left. As we went out of the room an exotic-looking, model-type girl rushed in, carrying flowers and more champagne.

'Darling! What have they done to you?'

Buster winked at me over her shoulder as we went out of the door.

We got a taxi home.

Cassie was still shaken by what had happened.

'Lukas must be completely paranoid,' she said in the taxi. 'To have someone beaten up just for asking questions.'

I nodded. 'Look what he did to us just for looking suspicious. And remember what he said to your mother, about things being at a crucial stage? I think this is the one time he can't afford any interference. Just the thought of it drives him crazy.'

When we got home, we went straight up to Cassie's flat and waited for her mother.

She arrived half an hour later, clutching a bulging briefcase.

'Just a quick snack and I've got to do some more work. There's another meeting with Lukas tomorrow.'

Cassie was unexpectedly firm. 'Never mind all that. Come into the study and get yourself a drink, we've got to talk to you.'

'Maybe later, darling –'

'No,' said Cassie. 'Now!'

Helen Sinclair's eyes widened in surprise, but she

followed us to the study, still carrying her briefcase.

Cassie sat her down and poured her a glass of wine.

'Now just listen. Weigh the evidence with that fine legal mind of yours.'

I started by telling her the full story of the return from Cambridge. 'That car ran us off the road deliberately, and Lukas was behind it. I bet the driver was one of the thugs who follow him around.'

'Look at the way he came rushing round here afterwards,' said Cassie. 'Full of concern about the accident. He knew it had happened because he set it up.'

'Why would he do such a thing?' demanded Cassie's mother. 'There's no proof he was involved.'

'There's a strong supposition,' I said. I told her Buster's story about the finance house chairman.

'Is that all?' asked her mother.

'No, there's more.' I told her about the results of Buster's other enquiries, and about the subsequent attack on him.

'It could have been a random mugging,' she said obstinately.

'By someone who warned him against asking questions?'

Mrs Sinclair was silent for a moment. 'It's pretty thin, isn't it? An accident in Cambridge, which could have been caused by some perfectly ordinary road hog. A rumour about an earlier road accident. An attack on some unfortunate businessman – all too common these days. It wouldn't stand up in court.'

'All the same, court is where it will end up,' said Cassie. 'Face it, Mum, your precious Lukas is a money-launderer, a professional criminal. He's planning some big-time scam, and you're helping him. He'll be caught in the end, and unless you pull out now, he'll drag you down with him. You'll end up in the dock, and very possibly in jail. It'll mean the end of your career and the ruin of your life – and mine as well.'

CHAPTER EIGHT

VANISHED

For a long moment Helen Sinclair just sat there, glaring furiously at us. It was easy to understand why. She was being told a lot of things she simply didn't want to hear. I remembered what Jim Broadbent had said back in Cambridge. '*When someone seems to have access to unlimited amounts of money, people don't always ask as many questions as they should.*'

When she spoke her voice sounded a little less certain. 'I've done nothing illegal . . .'

'Not knowingly, I'm sure,' I said. 'But suppose you've been acting on false information, forged papers? Isn't there a legal saying about ignorance being no excuse? Even if you escape prosecution, the scandal would ruin you. It wouldn't do much for Cassie or her father either!'

'Listen to him, Mum,' pleaded Cassie. 'You know we're not making it all up for the fun of it.'

Helen Sinclair sat silent for a moment longer. Then she said, 'All right, I'll tell you what I'll do. I'll look into things, ask a few more questions, make a few more checks. If I find the faintest sign of anything – unpleasant, I'll pull out of the deal immediately. Good enough?'

We both nodded. It was as good as we were going to get.

Cassie ran over to her mother and hugged her. Helen Sinclair hugged her back and I saw the real affection between them. Cassie's mother loved her work – but she loved her daughter even more. She pushed Cassie gently away.

'Now clear off, you, and let me get on. I've got a stack of work to do. More than ever, thanks to you two!'

Cassie and I left her to it, and went down to the Italian café for a celebration pizza.

'What do you think?' I asked, as we sat waiting for our food to arrive.

'I think we've done it,' said Cassie. 'Mum's pretty shrewd, and we've managed to make her suspicious. If there's anything wrong going on, she'll spot it and she'll be off like a scalded cat. She won't want any spots on her precious legal reputation.'

After our pizzas we chatted over coffee for a while.

'What do you want to do tomorrow?' I asked.

'I'm going clothes shopping in the morning.' She grinned. 'You can come if you like.'

I shuddered. 'No thanks.'

'See you around teatime, then. Come round and we can watch a video or go to the cinema.' She yawned. 'I think I'd better have an early night. All this excitement is wearing me out.'

I slept late the next morning, got up and had some burned toast and weak coffee served by our grim-faced housekeeper. I sorted out some laundry and dry-cleaning and made a feeble stab at tidying my room. I realised I was filling in time till I saw Cassie again, and thought how much I missed her, even after a few hours.

I wondered how she felt about me.

Early that afternoon, still thinking about Cassie, I started getting a strange feeling. It was like nothing I'd ever experienced before, and I wondered what was happening to me. Waves of emotion swept over me – fear, loss, panic – and a strong sense of Cassie, as though she was there in the room with me. It was all combined with a strange sense of dread, as though something terrible had happened to her.

I stood it until nearly four, and then went up to her flat and rang the bell, hoping desperately that she would answer the door. She didn't. Nobody did.

I went back to my own flat. The feeling came again, stronger than before.

I went back to Cassie's place at four thirty, at five and again at five thirty. Still nobody answered the door. I went back to my own place, seriously worried now. 'Teatime' was a vague term, but I reckoned five thirty was as late as it got.

I got the number of Sinclair Associates, Cassie's mother's firm, from Directory Enquiries and called them. I asked the receptionist to put me through to Helen Sinclair, giving my name and saying it was about her daughter Cassie.

I had to go through a couple of snooty secretaries – obviously Helen Sinclair was too important to talk to just anybody. Eventually she came on the line; her voice sounded tense and irritable.

'Yes, Ben, what is it? I'm in a meeting.'

'Sorry to bother you at work, Mrs Sinclair, but I'm a bit worried about Cassie. She was supposed to meet me around teatime but she hasn't turned up. It's almost six now and I was wondering –'

'Cassie's gone away,' interrupted her mother.

'Without telling me?' It was an instinctive reaction.

'There was no time, it was all arranged very quickly. I decided she'd be better away from London for a while.'

'Where is she? Can you give me an address or a telephone number?'

'She's gone abroad with a party of friends. They're touring. It was a snap decision.'

'Where?'

'I'm not quite sure where they're going first. I expect she'll write or call when they get settled. Sorry, Ben, I'll have to go now. I'm very busy.'

There was the click of the replaced receiver and then silence.

I started to dial again, but gave up the idea. She wouldn't tell me any more, probably wouldn't even speak to me.

I sat back in my chair and thought about what she'd told me. It simply didn't make sense.

It was plausible enough that Cassie's mother would decide to send her away for a while. Away from Lukas – away from me, come to that. I had a sneaking feeling she considered me a bad influence.

What I didn't believe in was this conveniently

vague group of touring friends. And there was no way she'd have set off straight from her shopping trip, with no luggage except a few bags of new clothes.

Since she'd hardly have taken her passport shopping with her, she would have had to come home to get it and pack. She knew I was at home, waiting for her. And I knew – not thought, but knew – that Cassie would have called me or, more likely, come over to see me before setting off abroad.

So her mother was lying.

Now, a lot of people – including my dad and most of my teachers – say I'm mentally lazy. But when there's a real crisis the old brain goes into overdrive. My mind was racing. It didn't take me very long to work out what had happened. The real problem was what to do about it.

There was one possible solution. It was something far out, a real long shot, but for the moment it was all I had.

I looked at my watch. I'd spoken to Cassie's mother at ten to six. It was just five to six now. Her offices were pretty close to her flat. If she left at once she could walk home in half an hour. If she took a taxi she could be home in about ten minutes. But I didn't think she would leave at once. She'd finish her meeting, clear up odds and ends, load up her briefcase.

According to Cassie, she usually got back at seven or seven thirty.

I reckoned I was safe until six thirty, which gave me half an hour.

Feeling more than a little foolish I went into my bedroom, drew the curtains and lay on my bed in the darkened room. I did my best to relax completely, and opened my mind to the feelings that had swept over me earlier.

Almost immediately the same sensations returned. Fear, panic, loss – and that same strange sensation of Cassie's presence. There was something else, too – a sense of urgency.

I lay back in the darkness and tried to let her reach me. Nothing happened at first, probably because I was trying too hard. But when I stopped concentrating and just let go, the feeling of being in contact with Cassie flooded in stronger than ever. And this time there was something else. I got a sudden picture of a broad, flowing river. Then everything faded away . . .

I sat up and looked at my watch. Quarter past six. I jumped up, left the flat and hurried over to Cassie's place. I rang the doorbell and, as I expected, there was no reply. I knew Cassie wouldn't be there, not now. And her mother wasn't back yet – which was all the better for my plan. I didn't think she'd want to talk to me again. I wasn't going to give her any choice.

I went back up the corridor, found a window with a view of the main foyer and hung about waiting. Quite a few returning residents passed by, and one or two of them glanced at me curiously. One old biddy looked so suspicious I was afraid she was going to call security.

I gave her my best boyish grin. 'Locked out,' I explained. 'Just waiting for Mum to get back.'

She gave me a sympathetic smile and passed by.

Ten minutes later, I saw Cassie's mother get out of a taxi.

I nipped back up the corridor, went past her flat and round the next corner. Feeling like some kind of cut-price James Bond, I lurked till I heard the lift doors opening, then peered cautiously round the corner. I saw her get out the key, open the door, start to go inside . . .

I belted along the corridor and followed her into the hallway of the flat before she could close the door. Then I kicked the door shut behind me.

She swung round, astonished and outraged. 'Ben! What do you think you're –'

I cut her off. 'Where's Cassie?'

'I told you, she's gone abroad visiting –'

'Stop lying!' I shouted. 'She's been kidnapped, hasn't she? Lukas has got her.'

She glared defiantly at me for a moment and then sort of slumped, almost collapsing.

'Yes,' she whispered. 'Lukas has got her.'

Chapter Nine

Rescue

I took her gently by the arm, led her into her study, sat her down and poured her a stiff drink – brandy this time.

I pulled up a chair and sat down close to her.

'All right, then, tell me about it.'

She sipped her drink for a moment, then sighed despondently. 'In a way it's all my fault. I had a meeting with Lukas and some of his people this morning, to go over the last stages of the takeover.'

'What takeover?'

She hesitated for a moment, then said, 'Lukas and his associates are planning a takeover of Barrington's Bank. They're offering an incredibly good price.'

I gave a sort of silent whistle. Barrington's wasn't the biggest bank in England, but it was one of the most prestigious. I'm not sure if it's got the Queen's account, but it certainly looks after most of her relatives. Not to mention most of the top people: everyone from lawyers to tycoons. With Barrington's in their hands the opportunities for money-laundering would be almost unlimited.

No wonder Lukas didn't want us spoiling his deal.

'When I was in the meeting I was thinking about all you two had said,' Helen Sinclair went on. 'There must have been something in my manner. Somehow Lukas picked up on it.'

Cassie wasn't the only one with amazing instincts, I thought. Lukas was like a wild animal, he could sense approaching danger. He'd sensed our suspicions, Cassie's and mine, when we met at the party. Now he'd sensed her mother's as well.

'I made matters worse by asking some rather pointed questions,' she continued. 'One or two references and guarantees hadn't come through as quickly as they should. I hinted that unless they turned up pretty quickly it might delay the deal.'

'What happened then?'

'Lukas adjourned the meeting until after lunch. He said he had to make a few phone calls, and then he'd give me a full answer to all my queries.'

'And did he?'

'As soon as the afternoon meeting started, there was a call for Lukas. He took it, said a few words in Hungarian, then passed me the phone. Cassie was on the line. She said two of Lukas's men had kidnapped her in Harrods. They just grabbed her arms and marched her out. I asked where she was and somebody put down the phone.'

'What did Lukas say then?'

Helen Sinclair drew a deep breath. 'He said if I ever want to see Cassie again, I've got to make sure the Barrington's takeover goes ahead as quickly as possible. If anyone queries the missing guarantees, I'm to say I've seen them and can swear that they're all in order. If I do that, Cassie will be well treated and released as soon as the deal is settled. If I tell the police, or anyone else, she'll be out of the country before anyone can find her. He said there's a good market for young girls like Cassie where he comes from.'

I could feel myself getting really furious and made an effort to stay calm.

'Anything else?'

She shook her head.

'Listen,' I said. 'This may seem a silly question, but it's really important. Is there anything to do with

Lukas that suggests a river to you? A deep, broad river, an estuary maybe?'

She gave me a baffled look. 'No . . . why?'

'I don't know if you're going to believe this,' I said slowly. 'I started getting weird feelings about Cassie this afternoon. Feelings that she was in trouble, and this image of a river. That's why I phoned you, I just wondered . . .'

She shook her head. 'I can't think of any–' She broke off. 'Wait a minute, he's got a boat!'

'What kind of boat?'

'A big cruiser, one of those floating gin palaces. It's called *Calypso*. He's really proud of it. He kept on asking me to go down there. He even showed me a photograph of it.'

'Where does he keep it?'

She frowned. 'Down at that big yachting centre in Essex. Burnham something. Burnham-on-Crouch!'

'Where exactly?'

'In some kind of marina, I think. He's too busy to go down there much. There are people to look after it. Do you think that's where he's keeping Cassie?'

'It's a possibility, isn't it? This was a spur of the moment job, so he had to improvise. It fits the threat about whisking her out of the country too. I don't suppose you know the name of the marina?'

'I'm afraid not.'

'Never mind, I'll find it.'

I jumped up and Mrs Sinclair jumped up as well.

'I'm coming with you.'

I shook my head. 'You'd better stay here in case Lukas calls. I'll call you myself the minute there's any news.'

Before she could argue I was out of the room and out of the flat. I sprinted back to my own place, went into Dad's study and called the executive car hire firm where he has an account I can use. I told them I wanted a fast car and a good driver right away.

I thought for a moment, then found a padded envelope, shoved a wad of blank paper inside and sealed it up with Sellotape. I got a marker pen and wrote MR LUKAS – URGENT in big black letters on the envelope.

I took a travel guide to Essex from Dad's reference shelf, went to my own room and grabbed the mobile I hardly ever use, then ran down to the main forecourt to wait for the car. A black BMW turned up a few minutes later. I gave the driver directions and we were off to the Essex coast.

I'd struck lucky with the driver. He was a big, tough, cheerful ex-Para called Bob. Dad always asked for him if he was carrying anything valuable.

As I'd hoped, the travel guide gave a list of marinas and their phone numbers. I used the mobile to call them one by one, asking for *Calypso*. I got lucky on my fifth try.

I gave Bob the address and we sped on our way. It's usually about a ninety-minute run down to the coast. We did it in just over an hour.

Typically of Lukas, the marina was one of the bigger and posher ones in the area. It was at the end of a rutted country lane and there was an open gate with a security guard in a booth beside it. I opened the car window and peered out as we approached. Through the gate I could see a broad stretch of open water, its banks lined with boats in deep-water moorings at the end of long wooden walkways. Most of them were big boxy things, what Cassie's mother had called floating gin palaces. They looked as if they never went to sea, and would probably capsize if they did. There didn't seem to be anybody about.

I leaned forward and spoke to Bob. 'Lend me your hat, just for a few minutes.'

He looked puzzled but passed it over.

'Turn the car and keep the engine running, will you? I hope to be back in a few minutes and I may want to leave in a hurry.' I paused and handed him the mobile. 'If I'm not back in half an hour, call the police. Tell them to look for me on *Calypso*.'

'If you're not back by then I'll come in and get you.'

He would too, I thought.

Bob gave me a worried look. 'Want me to come with you?'

I thought about it, then shook my head. 'I'll stand a better chance of getting a look round on my own. Who notices a delivery-boy?'

Totally baffled by now, Bob said, 'Suit yourself, squire.'

I jumped out of the car and put on the hat. It was a bit too big, so I tipped it to the back of my head. Clutching the envelope I went over to the booth. I held up the envelope and said, in my best cheeky-chappy voice, 'Letter for Mr Lukas's boat, *Calypso*.'

The guard was a tubby, middle-aged bloke in shirt-sleeves.

'Give it here, then.'

I shook my head. 'Can't be done, mate. Strict instructions. I'm to hand it over personal, to Mr Lukas or one of his staff, and get a signature.'

'Suit yourself. *Calypso*'s down there, at the end of that walkway.'

He pointed to a big, sleek cruiser at the end of its own walkway. This was a proper boat, one that could whisk an unwilling passenger over to the Continent.

'Mr Lukas ain't there, though,' he went on. 'A couple of his blokes just come down. Brought a girlfriend with them.'

I felt a sudden surge of hope.

Pulling my hat down low, I strolled along the wooden walkway towards *Calypso*. There was a row of portholes along the side and as I got nearer I saw a pale face looking out of one of them.

Cassie!

She pointed upwards, urgently. There was someone on the boat. I nodded and walked on. The walkway led to an entrance gate in the low railing that surrounded *Calypso*'s deck. Beyond it was a cabin. An open door showed steps leading downwards.

I jumped on board, glanced around and bellowed, 'Ahoy there!'

A voice from above called, 'Hey you! What you think you do?'

I looked up. A swarthy-looking man in a rumpled black suit and a white open-necked shirt was peering down at me from the cabin roof. It was one of Lukas's bodyguards, one of the three moustached thugs who followed him around. It was lucky for me it was the smallest one. I wouldn't have fancied tackling either of the others.

Pulling my cap down further over my face, I waved the envelope. 'Letter for Mr Lukas. Important business documents. I need a signature.'

'He not here.'

'Then you'll have to sign. Come on, mate, don't keep me hanging about.'

He started climbing down a metal ladder and I strolled casually over to the far side of the deck, gazing down at the water.

When I heard him coming up behind me, I turned and held out the envelope.

He took it and muttered, 'Where I sign?'

I pretended to fish in my pockets for pen and paper.

He was staring hard at me and suddenly he reached out and knocked the peaked cap from my head. 'You! I know you!'

He made a sudden rush at me. I jumped aside and he missed, staggering into the low railing round the deck. Before he could recover his balance I shoulder-charged him, sending him clean over the side. Without even waiting to see him hit the water I turned and ran for the main hatchway. I slid down a steep flight of stairs and ran along an oak-panelled corridor, yelling, 'Cassie! Cassie!'

I heard her voice. 'In here, in here!'

It came from behind a cabin door with a key in the

lock. I turned the key, opened the door and there was Cassie.

Before she could say anything I grabbed her arm and pulled her out of the cabin.

'Don't talk. Run!'

We ran back along the corridor, up the ladder, out on to the deck. A dripping form was just hauling itself over the side. 'Keep going, Cassie!' I shouted.

I dashed over and gave the man a shove that sent him straight back into the water. Then I followed Cassie off the boat. We sprinted down the walkway, running towards the astonished security guard.

He shouted, 'Hey!' and made a vague attempt to stop us, but we dodged him, ran out of the gates and jumped into the car, which was waiting, engine running.

'Home, please!' I shouted, and we sped away.

We sat back in the seat, gasping for breath.

Cassie grabbed both my hands, squeezing hard. 'I knew you'd come. I knew! I kept thinking about you, trying to reach you.'

'Message received, fortunately,' I said.

'How did you know where to come?'

We exchanged stories. I told her how I'd found her, with her mother's help.

She told me about being kidnapped in Harrods.

'It was the big one and the tall, thin one. They just grabbed my arms and marched me out. If anyone got in their way they shouted, "Shop-lifter! Shop-lifter!" I suppose people thought they were store detectives.'

They'd bundled her into a waiting car and driven her down to the marina.

'That skinny little chap was already there. He shoved me in a cabin and locked the door, then the two that had brought me just cleared off. The skinny one brought me some food and water, then just left me locked in there. So I lay on the bunk and tried to reach you.'

We had a lot to talk about and it wasn't until we were nearly home that I remembered my promise to call her mother. I got my mobile from the driver and dialled Cassie's number. After a few rings somebody picked up the telephone.

'Mrs Sinclair? It's Ben. I've got Cassie here, she's all right.'

But it wasn't Helen Sinclair who answered me. It was Lukas.

'I am sorry that Cassie is no longer enjoying our hospitality. However, her mother has now replaced her. She will see our project through, under my close personal supervision. Do not attempt to find her, she is far away. If you go to the police, or cause any trouble at all – you will never see her again.'

The telephone went dead.

CHAPTER TEN

CASSIE'S GIFT

Telling Cassie what had happened was one of the hardest things I've ever done, but she took the news amazingly well. In a quiet, determined voice she said, 'We've got to find her.'

'We will,' I said. 'We found you, and we'll find your mother.'

I was speaking a lot more confidently than I felt. I couldn't help feeling a certain reluctant admiration for Lukas. He'd moved with amazing speed. As soon as he learned he'd lost the daughter – the dripping thug must have telephoned him – he'd taken the mother. I felt that was partly my fault: I should have telephoned earlier.

How he thought Helen Sinclair could do her job as his captive was another matter. It might work, for just a few days. And he could still use the threat of harm to Cassie to control her.

We were silent for the remainder of the journey, both of us lost in thought. When we drew up outside Pennington Towers, I asked Bob to wait. I gave him a fiver and apologised for the loss of his hat, telling him to put the cost of a replacement on the bill.

'We'll probably be half an hour or so,' I said. 'There's a carpark round the back and a café if you want to grab a bite. Put that on the bill as well.'

As Bob drove away, Cassie and I headed for the lifts.

'Why did you ask the driver to wait?' asked Cassie.

'We'll need him when we go and get your mother.'

'We don't know where she is!'

'We will soon.'

This time I was almost as confident as I sounded. I had a plan.

'How?' demanded Cassie as we came out of the lift.

'It all depends on you, really.'

'I'll do anything, you know that.'

'Wait till you hear,' I said.

We went to my flat and got a couple of Cokes from the kitchen fridge and took them into my little study. Cassie sat down and I took a chair near her. This was going to be tricky.

'You remember when we first met,' I began. 'That business with the school coach crash?'

She nodded. 'It seems ages ago, but it's just a few days.'

'After that I did a bit of research on the Net – into the paranormal, psychic powers, that sort of thing.'

Cassie's eyes flashed. 'To find out how much of a weirdo I really was?'

Like I said, this was going to be tricky.

'No! Because I wanted to be your friend, and I needed to understand you better.'

'Oh,' she said. 'Sorry.'

'All this paranormal stuff has been researched, recorded, written up,' I said. 'Did you ever look into it?'

Cassie shook her head. 'I always hated the idea of it too much. Being different.'

'That flash you got when you touched the coach door is called psychometry,' I went on. 'The way you reached me when you were kidnapped is called a psychogram. A spirit message, a mental picture.'

Cassie sat, hunched and tense. 'I'd never done anything like that before. I needed to reach you so much . . . it just happened.' She shook her head wonderingly. 'I never realised this thing was a whole field of study. I thought it was just – me.'

'Don't be so vain,' I said. 'You're just a common-or-garden, everyday psychic. World's full of them!'

Cassie looked cross for a moment – then she looked pleased. Pleased and relieved. I had an almost irresistible urge to kiss her, but I didn't want to disturb her concentration – or mine!

'It feels good to be part of some kind of group,' she said softly. 'Even a weird group. Better than being a solitary freak.'

'You know about dowsing?' I asked. 'Water divining? Finding water, or buried pipes, even oil or minerals with a forked stick? It twitches in the dowser's hands over the right spot.'

Cassie nodded. 'I've heard of it.'

'There's a rarer version as well. Some people can dowse, or divine, using a pendulum over a map.' I paused. 'They can also find people.'

Cassie's eyes were filled with panic. 'Ben, I can't!'

'The coach crashed,' I reminded her. 'Lukas turned out to be a villain. You led me to the boat. How do you know till you try?'

She shook her head miserably. 'I can't. I can't.'

'Listen, Cassie,' I said urgently. 'This power of yours isn't a curse, not unless you make it one. Used properly, it's a gift. It's time you stopped being scared of it, learned to use it for good. And right now it's your mother's only chance.'

For a moment Cassie sat silent, shivering. Then, slowly, she straightened up. The panic faded from her face, to be replaced by a look of grim determination.

'All right. How do we begin?'

'Have you got anything we can use as a pendulum?'

Cassie reached into her T-shirt and pulled out a heart-shaped gold locket on the end of a long, thin gold chain.

'Will this do? Mum inherited it from her mum and passed it on to me.'

'Perfect!'

I went to my bookshelves and hauled out an atlas of Great Britain. I turned to the page showing the area around London.

'I reckon all that "somewhere far away" business was just a bluff,' I said. 'If he wants her to help with a scam in the City of London he can't be too far away. So let's start here.'

We spread out the atlas on the floor and Cassie held the locket over the map. For a moment it was still.

'Nothing's happening,' whispered Cassie.

'Relax. You're trying too hard. Relax and concentrate, both at the same time.'

Cassie drew a deep breath and sat, calm and still.

The locket began to swing in slow circles. The

circling turned into a swinging to and fro. Then the locket came to a halt. I bent down and studied the map. The locket was poised over a country town called St Neots, between Cambridge and Bedford.

I turned to a map of the area. Cassie swung the pendulum again, and it settled over a village called Little Chittering, just east of the town.

I stared down at the map in frustration. 'We can't search a whole village. We need more detail.' I stared round the room. 'Got it. My computer.'

I went over and switched it on. I searched through my collection of CD-ROMs until I found the one I was looking for, then slid it into the computer.

'What's that?' asked Cassie.

'Ordnance Survey maps of Great Britain,' I said. 'The really big-scale ones show every house, rock and tree!' I worked my way through the maps, scaling up till I found what I was looking for – a map of Little Chittering that showed every single house.

I printed it off and we spread it out on the floor. The pendulum circled, swung – and settled over a big house just outside the village.

'That's it,' I said. 'Let's go!'

We left the flat and hurried down to the restaurant, where we found Bob finishing off a plate of spaghetti.

I gave him the map and told him our next destination.

'Little Chittering, just off St Neots,' he said. 'No problem!'

Two hours later we were standing outside a big, gloomy house on the outskirts of Little Chittering. It was getting dark now, and the old house loomed darkly against the evening sky. We'd parked in a lay-by a little way back, and gone the rest of the way on foot.

I turned to Bob who'd insisted on coming with us.

'We think my friend's mother is being held in that house against her will,' I said.

Bob took it in his stride as usual. 'Why not phone the police, then?'

I tapped the mobile in my pocket. 'We will – but we want to make sure she's there first. We could use some extra muscle – are you on?'

'No problem!'

We crept up the drive. Light shone from behind heavily curtained windows.

'We need to be sure she's really in there,' I said. 'If we can get a look inside . . .'

We moved towards the downstairs front window. Cassie peered through a gap in the curtains. 'She's there!'

Through the gap you could see part of an old-fashioned sitting-room. At a roll-topped desk in the corner sat Cassie's mother, working on a pile of papers. Lukas sat in an armchair near by, watching her.

'Right,' I said. I took out my mobile, dialled nine, nine, nine and asked for the police.

'I want to report a kidnapping . . .'

The calm lady on the other end of the line listened to my story, took down the details and told me to wait and do nothing. Help was on the way.

I passed the message on to Cassie and Bob, and we settled down to wait.

Suddenly, the biggest of Lukas's three thugs came round the corner of the house and saw us hiding by the window.

He froze in astonishment and Bob leaped on him with a tiger-like rush. I saw Bob's arm chop down and the thug fell with no more than a grunt.

Even so, the grunt and the thud of the man's fall were enough to alert Lukas.

Peering through the gap in the curtain I saw that Lukas was looking suspiciously towards the window.

'He heard something,' whispered Cassie. 'He said he'd kill her if we interfered. We've got to get her out!'

I was feeling a sort of reckless excitement. I'd had enough of Lukas.

'How about the direct method?' I said.

There was a heavy garden bench close to the window. Bob and I picked it up, swung, and hurled it right through the glass.

There was a tremendous crash as the window exploded inwards against the heavy drapes. Cassie pulled back the curtains and yelled, 'Mum! Come on!'

Helen Sinclair didn't waste any time. She grabbed an armful of papers, ran across the room and hurdled through the shattered window. With a roar of rage, Lukas jumped up and rushed after her.

As he appeared at the window, Bob stepped forward and delivered an uppercut that knocked him right back into the room.

I looked inside and saw a dazed Lukas struggling to his feet. I wanted him to know I was there, that I'd beaten him.

'Take that, my Hungarian friend!' I yelled.

Cassie tugged at my arm. 'Ben, come on! Run!'

We turned and fled towards the gate.

Suddenly a bedraggled, skinny figure appeared in front of us. It was the thug from the boat. Bob stiff-armed him away almost casually, and he staggered backwards into an ornamental pond with a yell and a splash. It just wasn't his day.

We ran down the lane and piled into the car. Bob slid calmly behind the wheel.

'Where to, guv? London?'

I had a sudden flash of inspiration. 'No, Cambridge.'

Not even Lukas would dare to disturb the calm of a Cambridge college, I thought hysterically. If he turned up with his trio of armed thugs, Professor Sinclair could just sport his oak . . .

That was almost the end of it.

We all turned up in Professor Sinclair's room, interrupting a peaceful evening's chess with Jim Broadbent. When he heard our story his face darkened with anger and he grabbed the telephone.

What happened next was a fine example of the Establishment in action. Between the two of them, Professor and Mrs Sinclair had a lot of clout, and they used it all.

The police were called – not the local bobby on a bike, but the Chief Inspector. Cassie and her mother made statements about their respective kidnappings, and I made a supporting statement as well.

We left out the psychic elements of both rescues, implying that both Cassie and her mother had somehow managed to get messages out.

The Chief Inspector went off to find a magistrate, and warrants were issued for the arrest of Lukas and his men on charges of kidnapping and fraud. Apparently

Cassie's mother had grabbed some incriminating documents as she escaped.

There had been nobody at the old house when the police arrived in answer to my nine-nine-nine call, but Lukas and his men were scooped up in Essex by an armed Special Patrol Group as they tried to reach their boat. They were arrested, committed for trial, and later released on bail for enormous sums – no problem to Lukas, of course.

While all this was going on, Cassie, her mother and I all stayed with Professor Sinclair in the guest rooms at the college. It seemed a good idea to keep out of the way. As I told Jim Broadbent, I wasn't crazy about the idea of running into Lukas while he was wandering about London on bail.

He smiled. 'I shouldn't worry. He won't be wandering around for long.'

'You mean he'll escape?'

He shook his head. 'Our friend Lukas was entrusted with a very important financial operation. He screwed it up badly, largely through arrogance and recklessness – with a little help from you and Cassie, of course. There's been a lot of bad publicity about foreign crooks operating in Britain. Controls are being tightened up. There are some very unforgiving people in the Russian mafia.'

Next day Lukas came out of a late-night meeting with his lawyer, got in his Porsche and switched on the engine. The car exploded. It was sheer good luck that the street was empty. One of his men, the big one, was in the car with him. The tall one and the little scrawny one vanished and were never seen again.

I wondered if they'd planted the bomb.

Half-term came to an end and Cassie and I went back to school.

Cassie's settled in really well this term; she's a lot more relaxed and confident now. She's becoming one of the most popular girls in the school. I get a lot of teasing from my friends about my glamorous new girlfriend. I play it cool and say we're just good friends. Unfortunately that's true – though maybe one day . . .

My dad came home from his trip and said he hoped I hadn't been too bored spending the half-term holiday alone with the housekeeper . . .

I don't see quite as much of Cassie as I did in those very early days. But we're still best friends, and I find her as fascinating as ever. Mostly she's just Cassie, great fun to be with.

But sometimes . . .

Sometimes she freezes, just for a moment, and gets this far away, abstracted look in her big green eyes, and I wonder what she's seeing that the rest of us can't.

One of these days, when she needs my help again, I expect I'll find out.

I'm looking forward to it.

Also available from Piccadilly Press, by
TERRANCE DICKS

Suddenly a man in a black uniform appeared, hurrying down the corridor towards them. He had heavy, brutal features and he had a holstered pistol at his belt. He was a sinister, frightening figure and Sarah saw that Tom was staring at him in horrified disbelief.

'Oh no!' he whispered. 'It can't be . . .'

'Can't be what?'

'SS,' muttered Tom.

The year is 2015, and the transporter has malfunctioned, reassembling Tom and Sarah in a parallel universe – one in which the Nazis have won World War II. It's a world of soldiers, guns and salutes, of work-camps and swift executions. On the run from the SS and unable to trust anyone, they must try to find a way back to their own universe . . .

"The action is satisfyingly frantic . . . (readers) will respond to Dicks' punchy style and relish the neat twist teasingly placed at the very end of the novel." Books for Keeps

Also available from Piccadilly Press, by
TERRANCE DICKS

'Sarah!' Tom shouted as he clung to the flooded rubble. 'Sarah? Where are you?'

He tried to peer through the choking mists and gain his bearings in this strange, hostile landscape.

Tom and Sarah arrive in a parallel universe, many years from now, where disaster reigns. The planet has been ruined by man's pillaging and pollution. Cities are under water, virulent plagues have killed much of the population, genetically mutated crops have destroyed agriculture and giant rats roam the countryside.

Civilisation has collapsed and the survivors battle against each other. Tom and Sarah must use all their combined courage to survive and escape home before it is too late.

Also available from Piccadilly Press, by
TERRANCE DICKS

THE UNEXPLAINED SERIES

The huge, eerie statues on Easter Island have always been one of the world's great mysteries. But now they have started moving and the scientific world is in uproar. What is happening? Is this some sort of supernatural event guided by alien hands?

When a scientific researcher is killed by one of the statues, Matt and his father are once again called upon to investigate a mystery that no on else is able to understand . . .

". . . fear addicts are starting to hunt out Terrance Dicks's series The Unexplained." The Sunday Times

". . . well-written and original." SFX magazine

Also available from Piccadilly Press, by
TERRANCE DICKS

THE UNEXPLAINED SERIES

Sinister deaths take Matt and Professor Stirling to Romania, close to the war-torn Balkans. But it isn't politics that draws Matt and his father to this remote spot.

Blood-drained corpses are being found in this region of Romania known as Transylvania. Can it be just a village feud? Or has a more ancient evil returned?

". . . A tale packed with tension and rich in historical detail."
100 Best Books 1999, Book Trust

If you would like more information about books available from Piccadilly Press and how to order them, please contact us at:

Piccadilly Press Ltd.
5 Castle Road
London
NW1 8PR

Tel: 020 7267 4492
Fax: 020 7267 4493